THIRTEEN YEARS WITH ZACORI

G. MADDOX

Thirteen Years With Zacori

Copyright 2015 © Gregory Maddox

I would like to dedicate this book to my daughters Leila and Meagan.
You have inspired me in every way to not only
reach for the stars, but also be a better man and father.
I live, love and breath for you. Thank you for completing me.
Love Dad

Chapter 1

Life before Zacori

It's a beautiful afternoon in New York City; the sun is bright and the streets are full with spirit. A young woman named Veronica sits in a small café located in the West Village. Today is no different from any other she has spent time there having a cup of her favorite coffee and looking at the classifieds. Things haven't been the best for her since she came from her native Ghana six years ago. With a high school diploma from back home, she has been able to attend community college and receive an associate degree in business. Her English hadn't been the best, but it's now good enough to land her part-time work with temp agencies. It isn't much, but enough to send a few dollars home after paying her bills and saving what she can out of the pennies that are left.

As she sips her coffee looking through job listings, she can only shake her head in disappointment looking at the available positions. *Cashier. No! Mechanic. Never! Dishwasher … I may be broke, but there are just certain things I can't do,* she thinks.

Her melancholy mood reflects the hardships she's faced like many other immigrants migrating to the U.S at a young age, working extra hard in an effort to find a future in the land of milk and honey to support the loved ones left behind. Veronica was once sold on the slogan, "If you can make it in New York, you can make it anywhere," but it didn't take long for her to face the reality of homeless people living on the street and the underlying racism usually disguised by smiles, which led her to believe segregation was still in some ways a major problem in the U.S.

She slowly folds the paper in disappointment, taking a deep, slow breath and looking at the ceiling as if to ask God *WHY*, but in the back of her mind she is truly afraid of the answer.

The door of the café swings open as a young woman dressed in athletic gear and pushing a stroller enters. As the woman walks to the counter to order, she parks the stroller adjacent to Veronica, who glances down at the child and smiles as his big blue eyes remain fixed on her with a look of curiosity and amazement. He has the rosiest cheeks she has ever seen, and a scarf wrapped around his neck so high only his upper cheeks and small bubbles of nasal discharge can be seen.

Veronica tries to ignore the child as much as she can, but he won't look away, so she softly waves and whispers, "Hello cutie. What's your name?"

He quickly places his hands over his face, smiling at her between his fingers. Slowly gliding his hands down, he watches Veronica in anticipation of her next move. Keeping a playful eye on him, she lays the paper down and says, "BOO!"

As he slumps down in his stroller laughing hysterically and blushing, his cheeks become even redder. At this moment, all the stress and worries of Veronica's day just pass by as she marvels at the innocence of this child. The sudden movement of his rocking in the stroller catches the attention of the mother, who looks down at her son gingerly laughing at Veronica.

"Zacori, are you bothering this young lady?" she asks.

"No, it's OK. Believe it or not, he actually just made my day look a whole lot brighter," says Veronica. She extends her index finger toward Zacori, who immediately grabs it with his tiny hands. "Wow! What a strong grip you have, sir. You are so adorable!"

"Yes, he is a bundle of joy," the mother says before introducing herself. "Hi! My name is Linda, and you have already met my son, Zacori."

"Veronica. Nice to meet you," she says, extending her hand.

"Do you have any kids?" Linda asks.

"No! Well, not yet anyway. I guess I'm still trying to find the right guy and have all my little duckies in line, you know."

"Well, let me give you some advice. First, you're never going to be ready for it. And second, as far as men go, not only will we never have enough time in a day, week or year, but this is lifetime is too short." The two ladies begin to laugh softly.

"It can't be that bad; I see you're married," Veronica gestures at the enormous ring on Linda's hand.

"I guess I'm pretty lucky with my husband. God forbid if I had to experience this dating scene now. Excuse me one second," says Linda, who has turned her attention to the cashier to retrieve her change. Veronica kneels back down to Zacori and places her hand on his little cap. As Linda turns again, she fumbles her coffee, which lands directly on Veronica's hands.

Veronica quickly jumps up, obviously in pain from the heat. The two of them begin using napkins to wipe the hot coffee off of her.

"I am so sorry!" cries Linda in deep concern. "Let me see your hands. Are they burned? I am so sorry this happened," she repeats.

"It'll be OK, trust me. I'm just happy it was my hand instead of his face. That would have been devastating," says Veronica.

Linda kneels down and takes off Zacori's hat to give him a thorough check as she wipes the coffee residue from his jacket. Reaching into her purse, she apologizes again and asks if she can do anything to help.

"Please believe me; I'm fine," Veronica responds.

They pause for a minute in hesitation, looking down at Zacori smiling at the two of them. The ladies are ready to part ways, but neither wants to be the first to do so.

"Well, I guess we should be going now, Zacori. Say goodbye to the nice lady."

Veronica bends down to Zacori. "It was such a pleasure meeting you, and thank you for making my day," she says to the cherry-cheeked toddler in the stroller. She stands and shakes Linda's hand.

"Are you sure I can't buy you a cup of coffee or something?" Linda asks.

"No! I'm going to just finish reading my paper, and then I will head out. Another cup of coffee may have me bouncing around this city," laughs Veronica.

As Linda begins to exit the café, Zacori extends his arms toward Veronica as if he wants her to pick him up. Upon realizing she won't, he begins crying and kicking his tiny legs in the stroller. Linda smiles at Veronica. "I have never seen him act this way before," she marvels.

Veronica sits back down, waving her last goodbye before watching them fade away into the distance. *Never a dull moment in this city*, she thinks to herself. She glances out the window, looking into the busy street as people pass by. Families strolling through the park, couples holding hands while pushing strollers and kids playing with the earth-tone colors of fall decorating the scenery give Veronica warm memories of the times she spent with her family back home.

Rubbing her hands into her face before glancing back in the classifieds, Veronica tries to hold back the tears building up in her eyes. *I really have to get it together; but I just don't know what I'm going to do,* she thinks, placing a line through all job listings she has no interest in until she reaches the bottom of the page. *What is this? Fabric designer – this doesn't sound too bad. I like clothes. I've got style. Why not?* She pulls out her cell phone, dialing the number with nerves taking over her stomach as it rings. After three rings, a receptionist answers.

"Fashion House! How may I direct your call?"

"Yes, I'm calling about the position posted in today's paper. Is it still available? And if so, is it possible to fax or e-mail my resume?"

"Sure. We actually have an open interview policy, and there is an opening on Thursday at ten o'clock if you're interested. All I would need from you is your name and a phone number where we can reach you, if there are any changes."

After exchanging the necessary information and receiving directions, Veronica places the phone down with excitement and looks toward the sky to thank God for his blessing.

She jumps up with excitement and screams YES, knocking her cup of coffee over on the table. As she quickly tries to clean it up, the waitress walks over and begins to pour her another cup shaking her head and smiling. Veronica continues cleaning the table and apologizing.

Chapter 2

The clock reads 7 a.m. Veronica lies in bed with her eyes open, excited but nervous about her interview today. The alarm rings, playing Whitney Houston's "I'm Every Woman" before she glides her fingers over to turn it off and stretch, letting out a thunderous yawn. Getting out of bed, she moves toward the window for her daily routine, kneeling on the floor with her face to the sky to begin her prayer:

> *Good morning God!*
> *Today is the day I come to you with thanks.*
> *Thank YOU for the air placed in my lungs.*
> *Thank YOU for the health of my family and friends. I thank YOU for waking me this morning to start anew on this blessed earth. I pray that YOU guide me through this day with patience and understanding and without confusion. This is the first day of my new beginning, the day that my struggle ends. YOU know my heart, YOU know who I am. Thank YOU for life, love and building me into the woman that I am today and will be tomorrow, with your grace. I love YOU. I need YOU. I appreciate YOU hearing my voice this morning. Amen.*

She sits in silence, becoming so emotional that tears begin to fall from her eyes. As she kisses her hands before raising them to the sky, sunlight begins to creep its way through the window, making her tears look like liquid crystals flowing down her brown skin. She smiles with joy before opening her eyes and whispering a quick thank you.

The interview with Fabric House for a designer position is at ten o'clock. Pulling out her nicely pressed business suit and giving it another look over, she begins to get prepared. Deep in her heart she knows that on this day her luck is going to change majorly. Every interview and opportunity is big for her. Looked upon as the person to help everyone back home, she has a sister who she feels deserves a great future and is raising money to bring her to the U.S. for a better education. Having watched her parents struggle so hard doing the best they could to send her to school while her brothers stayed home to work on the farm with only a grade school education overwhelmed with her guilt. At times, she blamed herself for their ignorance.

After getting out of the shower, she gets dressed and gathers her belongings to head out of the door. Money these days is scarce, but she's been able to barely come up with enough fare to go and return without interfering with the bill money. Even though she has close to nothing, things still aren't hard enough for her to ask for handouts or resort to public assistance, something her pride would never let her do.

An hour has passed when Veronica arrives at the train stop. Her watch reads 9:30 a.m. and being late is not an option at this point, as it was instilled in her that the first impression is always a lasting one. Looking up and down the block for landmarks to guide her to the location, she remembers what the receptionist said about walking toward the water.

Moments later, she arrives in front of the building and gives herself one last look before entering the front door. Taking a deep breath before walking up the steps, Veronica gives herself a little pep talk. *You can do this, girl! You can do this!*

The receptionist sits below a huge fabric sign that reads "Fabric House," which Veronica finds very unique.

"Hello! My name is Veronica Owuso, and I have an interview today at ten o'clock."

"Yes! I believe I remember talking to you on Tuesday. If you could just have a seat, you will be called in as soon as Mr. Burns is ready to see you," the receptionist says.

Veronica begins to get nervous as she waits and glances at the magazines on the table, each involving high-powered business, which is a good sign that the owner is not planning on failing. After a few minutes have passed, a tall, slender woman comes from the back and calls Veronica's name. Taking a deep breath and crossing her fingers before standing, she acknowledges the woman by shaking her hand and then follows her toward the back. As they travel down the hallway, Veronica gets additional directions to the whereabouts of the interviewer.

"If you just go down the hallway, you will see Mr. Burns' office; he's expecting you," the woman says. "Good luck!"

Veronica heads down the corridor looking at the designs hanging on the wall, which were manufactured by the company. There are also pictures of who she assumes is Mr. Burns with other businessmen of Asian descent. She arrives at the office and knocks on the door. A male voice answers, "Come in."

As she enters the office overlooking the New York skyline, Mr. Burns is on the phone and gestures for Veronica to have a seat. Just looking around the office, she can only imagine the business opportunities that could arise from this job, taking in the Fortune 500 magazine cover hanging in the frame, golf trophies and unique artifacts that only a person who has traveled the world and knows the finer things in life could appreciate. Mr. Burns hangs up the phone and speaks.

"I'm sorry for keeping you waiting. I had a really important phone call that needed my attention. My name is Mr. Burns and I am the CEO of the Fabric House. Have you any experience in the fabric industry?" he asks, looking down at the resume.

"Before you answer that, why don't you tell me something about yourself?"

"My name is Veronica Owuso and I'm from Ghana originally."

"Beautiful country – I have visited there many times before myself," says Mr. Burns.

"Thank you! Well, I'm 29 years old, and I moved to New York almost four years ago searching for better opportunities to one-day help my family at home. I have received my associate degree in business and am currently pursuing my bachelor's. I'm ambitious, open-minded for change, and eager to become grounded with a job where I can not only grow, but also join a family."

"So you feel that a company is equivalent to a family?"

"In my opinion, a business that remains successful is only because the leaders are like parents. They guide firmly but understand that they are dealing with the emotions of others."

As Veronica continues talking, Mr. Burns sits in the chair with his hand on his chin, carefully listening to her speak. He nods his head in agreement before stopping her. "Looking at your resume, I see that you don't have any experience in fashion. But I must tell you, so far I am very impressed with the way you carry yourself and the confidence in your voice. I usually don't make decisions this quickly about hiring somebody, but I'm willing to offer you a position if you can answer this one question. I need you to give me your most HONEST answer, not what you think I want to hear," he says.

"OK!" Veronica responds nervously.

"Why should I hire you?"

Veronica pauses for a minute, deep in thought.

"There is no rush to give me an answer, as long as it is the truth."

"The most honest answer I can give you is that there are too many reasons why I need this job. Besides the fact that I had to scrap up change to get here, I know what it's like to have nothing. I am the only woman in my family with an education. I came here with the dream to help and educate the ones I left behind, and whether I'm hired today or next year, I will never quit until I become successful. That's my honest answer." Veronica sits back in the chair and takes a deep breath before folding her hands on her lap.

Mr. Burns nods his head in agreement. "I must tell you, I have interviewed hundreds of people since becoming a boss, but that was the most unique and truthful answer I've ever heard. It's that drive that I need in this company. I'm going to ask you to wait outside in the waiting area, and the receptionist will give you the details," he says.

"OK! It was a pleasure meeting you. And thank you for the chance for an interview," she says before standing while extending her hand.

"It was a pleasure meeting you, and thank you for coming in," Mr. Burns responds.

As Veronica heads down the hallway to the waiting area where the receptionist sits, she questions herself reflecting back on the interview, telling herself if it's meant to be it will be. The receptionist notices her approaching and gestures that Veronica sits in the chair while see finishes her conversation on the phone.

"Yes, sir! I will make sure all the proper paperwork is in line and on your desk immediately, sir. Excuse me, Veronica. I'll just ask you to finish some paperwork before you leave." The receptionist leans down to her desk drawer.

"Sure, no problem," Veronica answers.

The receptionist places a folder on the desk before handing it to Veronica to look over the documents inside. The front cover of the folder reads NEW EMPLOYEE ORIENTATION. "Is this for me? Does this mean I have the job?" she asks, trying not to seem so excited.

"Yes it is. Mr. Burns has decided he wants you to be part of his team, immediately. Congratulations, and welcome to the Fashion House!"

"YES!" shouts Veronica.

"Wow!" says the receptionist as she recognizes the emotions Veronica is expressing. "I know exactly how you feel. It's OK. We just have some documents that need to be filled out to create a file for you. Is there anything at this time that will prevent you from coming on board?"

"Not that I can think of at this time. Oh wait! I am in the process of getting my citizenship. Will that interfere with anything?" Veronica asks.

"I don't think so. We are a very equal opportunity employment cooperation, so it should be fine," the receptionist assures her.

"I'm sorry; I just got a little excited," says Veronica. "Thank you."

"If you have any questions, please feel free to ask. Once you finish, you can give it back to me and I will let you know your start date. Welcome aboard! My name is Theresa."

After finishing the necessary paperwork, Veronica exits the building with a new outlook on life. She is not only securing her financial future, but also becoming part of an established business that will give her the opportunity to utilize her degree. The only thing on her mind is making it home to express to her family the wonderful news. So excited upon finally arriving home, she pulls the calling card from her purse, grabs the phone and begins to dial the number, not even taking the time to remove her coat. After the second ring, Veronica's mom picks up the phone.

"Hello?"

"Hi, Mommy! It's me, Veronica."

"How are you, my dear? I was just thinking about you. Everything OK?" Mom asks.

"Actually things were getting really rough, but I was able to get a much better job today. I really feel that things are about to turn around now. I prayed so much for this to happen, and today it did."

"We've always been so proud of you, Veronica. You have so much strength and drive in you. If there is anything that I'm sure of, it is that you will always find a way. And I know that you are blessed in so many ways. I want to thank you for all you strive to do."

"Why are you thanking me?" Veronica asks.

"One day when you have children, you will understand why a parent thanks their child at times," her mother says.

"OK, Mom; I understand. Well, I just wanted to call and tell you the good news. I will call you and Dad again as soon as I can. How is Dad?"

"He's good, my dear. I will let him know that you called and did ask for him. Be careful, and we love you."

"I know, Mom. Love you guys too!"

After Veronica hangs up the phone, she sits on the couch and thinks of what to do next, still excited about the new venture she's about to embark on. Quickly jumping off the couch, she races toward her room and lifts up her mattress, where her emergency money is stored. *I know I shouldn't spend this on something other than what I need, but I have worked so hard in budgeting and trying to find a job. I deserve to enjoy myself,* she thinks. *I'm going out tonight and have a glass of wine or two. I deserve it.* She turns the radio up and looks in the closet to pick out an outfit before making her way out the door.

Chapter 3

Anyone who has ever visited New York knows there's no nightlife like it in the world. It's the kind of place where you can meet the person of your dreams, or all your dreams can come crashing in the blink of an eye. Veronica is more than ready to take advantage of the night as she strolls gingerly down the street looking for a lounge called Mocha. A Ghanaian owns it, so she knows that the vibe and energy will be exactly what she needs to have a good time.

Once she arrives at Houston and Varick streets, the bright lights from the harness immediately catch her attention. Not discouraged by the line extending to the corner, Veronica places herself in perfect position to ensure her entrance. After twenty minutes on li she finally enters. Immediately she is overwhelmed by the Afrocentric décor, which resembles a royal palace. The amazingly bright-colored walls with beautiful sculptured artifacts made of mahogany wood along the sides' gives her the feeling of being home. Now she understands why this is such a popular place within the African community.

As she walks through the crowd feeling out the place, she suddenly feels a hand softly tap her arm. Knowing how men can be, especially in a social environment after a few drinks, she ignores the gentleman with a smile not to seem rude and makes her way to the bar.

"What can I help you with today?" asks the bartender kindly.

"I would like a white wine, preferably a Riesling if you have," says Veronica.

While the bartender fixes her drink, the same gentleman who brushed her arm approaches the bar, takes a seat next to her and smiles. She glances at him briefly, not showing much interest but avoiding being disrespectful. Her drink finally arrives, and she searches through her purse to pay.

"Please allow me to take care of that for you," he says.

"Thank you. But it's OK," she responds.

"No! It will be my pleasure. I would feel so bad if you refused to allow me to be a gentleman. What would my mother say? She would slap my head if I didn't do this," he says as he smiles innocently.

She knows it might be virtually impossible to get rid of him after this drink, but keeping the twenty dollars in her pocket is more important. "Thank you. This is very nice of you," she says.

"My name is Osogwa. May I ask yours?"

"I'm Veronica," she answers.

An hour has gone by, and it seems that Veronica and Osogwa are having a great conversation. It wasn't part of the original plan, but he is very respectful of her space and the conversation is ongoing. Hesitant to dance, they playfully nod their heads to the beat of the music. Suddenly, the sound of native drums erupts into the atmosphere and the aura of the club changes immediately. The rhythm of the live instruments makes the people move while the pounding of drums rattles the floor. As much as Veronica wants to resist, she can no longer hold it in. Raising her arms as if possessed by her ancestors, she moves her hips side to side seductively. Osogwa gently places his hands upon her hips and moves to her lead.

As the music plays and the people scream the sounds of the tribal tongue, Veronica becomes so overwhelmed with joy that she never realizes the grasp of Osogwa's hands on her body. For the first time since leaving Africa, she felt as if home has come to her. After the band finishes their set, the crowd erupts with cheers and applauds for what seems like eternity to show their appreciation. Veronica looks down at her watch, which reads 3:45 a.m.

"Oh my goodness! I didn't realize that it was so late. I really should be heading home," she says.

"Let me walk you to your car?" Osogwa asks.

"Actually I took the train, but you can walk me to the door if you'd like," she says.

They retrieve their coats from the coat check and exit the club. Shivering from the New York cold, Veronica rubs her hands and fixes her jacket to fit her more snugly. Osogwa places his jacket around her shoulders for added warmth.

"Thank you," she says.

"You know, it's pretty late. Why don't you let me offer you a ride home? Or better yet, you can come to my home," he suggests, grasping her shoulders firmly.

"Wow! That's a little too suggestive for me. I had a great time with you; I will admit that. But I was thinking more along the lines of exchanging numbers and seeing how things can go slowly," she says.

"I'll respect that. How about a goodnight kiss?" he asks, placing his hands at her side. She nervously laughs and escapes his grasp.

"I think that's a little inappropriate. I'm sorry if you got the wrong impression, so here's your jacket. Thank you for a nice time," she says.

"Really? For all the money I spent on you tonight, I deserve a little more than a hug, don't you think?" He grabs her so firmly that Veronica's face suddenly turns to fear. "I see the kind of woman you are. You come to the club, have a man spend a lot of money and think it's just fine to lead him on. You are going to do a little more tonight, believe me," he says forcefully advancing himself against her body.

Veronica repeatedly tells him to stop as Osogwa muffles her mouth while dragging her slowly to the ground in the darkly shaded alleyway. All Veronica can do is try to force him off, but it only makes him more aggressive.

"I guess we are going to do this the hard way," he growls before plowing his fist twice into her face. The blows are so forceful that she becomes dazed and can only feel the pressure continuing to beat on her face, which becomes numb to the pain after a few more blows. She can only hear the muffled sounds of bone cracking as the abuse continues.

It takes all the strength she has left to beg him "Please wear a condom!" He begins to rip off her dress and unzip his slacks, as Veronica lies helpless. At this point she closes her eyes and surrenders to stop the beating, realizing she will be the victim of what she feels is the worst thing a woman can face: rape. She feels a sudden thump as Osogwa's body falls forcefully to her side. She hurries to get herself together as a stranger stands over Osogwa, viciously kicking him in the ribs and face until his blood runs down the alley like water in a small creek. She wants to run, but is too weak and dizzy to stand, so she sits covering herself up. As she looks on at the aggressor now being manhandled, in the back of her mind she enjoys seeing the pain and fear in his eyes as he is left with no choice but to accept what is forcefully being brought on him. It is her revenge, watching him being beat like the animal he is.

The gentleman looks over to Veronica and asks, "Are you OK?" He extends his hands to help her up, but she only flinches as her nerves and broken trust make her hesitant to accept anything from a man. "Please, let me help you up. I am not here to hurt you. My friend has already alerted the police and they are on their way. I will remain with you to keep you safe until they come." Veronica slowly brings herself off the ground and begins to get herself together. She places her hand against her eye to feel the damage Osogwa's punches have caused.

"Oh my God! I can't believe this just happened!" she cries out, shaking with fear.

"Do you want to go to the hospital?" he asks as he takes off his blazer and places it over her shoulders. The sound of police sirens begins to fill the air, letting them know the authorities are on their way. "Excuse me one moment," he says. He walks over to Osogwa, who is lying there moaning, and gives him a few more assuring blows to let him know he has not gotten off the hook yet.

"Is there anything I can do for you?" he asks Veronica.

"No, I'm fine! Thank you," she says.

The police arrive on the scene and approach them standing under the light pole. They ask Veronica if she is OK and let her know the ambulance will be there soon. "Can you give us a description of the suspect?" the police ask.

"Well he doesn't look the same as before, but he's lying over there," the stranger says. I had to subdue him in order to stop him from raping her. I'm willing to answer any questions you may have for me."

The police walk over to Osogwa and help him to his feet as he screams; "It was I who tried to stop him from beating her. He is her pimp and they were trying to solicit me. When I didn't want to participate, they beat me like this!" Veronica walks over to him and slaps him in the face as hard as she can.

"That is far from the truth! This animal tore off my clothes and forced himself upon me. I met him in the club, and after a few drinks he thought I owed him more. I was trying to leave before he attacked me, forcing me to the ground and punching me in the face, until this man risked his life to save mine," she explains.

"Don't worry, ma'am! We believe you," one officer says. They take Osogwa immediately into custody. The stranger remains on the scene until Veronica is placed in the ambulance. He waves goodbye to her, and she returns a wave back, silently thanking him. Now in the ambulance, she realizes she didn't even get his name.

Chapter 4

Three weeks have passed since that almost-fatal night at the club. Veronica's face has healed up very well, and it's her first day on the new job. She is escorted by Mr. Burns' assistant through the factory and remains silent as she observes her new home away from home. It doesn't take her much time to notice that the majority of the workers are of Asian descent and keep their heads buried on the fabric tables in front of them. Periodically they look up or speak to the workers next to them, but their observed work habits are almost robotic. Arriving at the cubicle assigned to her, she looks at the beautiful fabrics neatly placed on the table. Still not sure of her responsibilities but filled with the excitement of starting a new job, Veronica reasons that she will just have to figure things out as she goes along. Mr. Burns approaches to greet her.

"Good morning, Veronica. I did a lot of thinking after you left the interview, and I decided to start you at a different position. I understand it may be a little challenging initially, but I think it's perfect for you," says Mr. Burns.

"Sure!" Veronica responds.

"It's nothing that I feel you won't be able to handle. I will actually be starting you out as a fabric analyst, and your main responsibility will be to make sure that the product has the proper pattern before going to the floor for processing," he states.

"Well, thank you sir. I'm honored!"

"The position can be challenging, but it also has a lot of room for growth. The reports must be very accurate, and most of all, on time."

"I totally understand. And sir, if I could just take this opportunity to thank you for …"

"Believe it or not I see something in you that made me feel confident in choosing you. Just don't let me down," he says jokingly. "Get settled, look over your manual, and welcome!" He places his cigar back in his mouth and walks off.

Veronica sits down and takes a deep breath before opening the manual that is possibly heavier than she is. After a few hours have passed, she continues reading while occasionally looking up at the other ladies in the office, who have not said a word to her or each other.

"Most of them don't speak English. That's why it's so quiet," a voice says.

Veronica looks over to a middle-aged Caucasian woman sitting across from her. "Hi. My name is Veronica," she says.

"Agnes."

"Is it always like this here? Today is my first day and I'm trying to get a vibe from the place, but it seems so distant and a bit cold."

"It's like this now. When I first started here many years ago, we were like a family. Now it has been such a difficult time of — how can I say it — change? It's really just an effort to save money, bringing in all these – well, you know!" Agnes says, making hand motions and mysteriously looking around as she waits for Veronica to fill in the blanks.

Veronica sits confused looking at Agnes, knowing in the back of her mind what she's trying to insinuate, but refusing to entertain the thought. "What are you exactly trying to say?" she asks.

"Come on. Cheap labor workers, American dream chasers?" says Agnes.

"Wow. That's a very serious accusation you're making. I hope that's not true, because believe it or not I'm also a foreigner," Veronica explains.

"Yeah, but you're not like them you know! You're..." Agnes pauses.

"Black!" suggests Veronica.

"Exactly! Our people are the real ones who deserve to progress in this society. Especially what your people have been through," says Agnes.

"OK! On that note, I think I will get back to this manual. But thank you for the insight," states Veronica. She turns back in her chair and shakes her head, amazed at the comments made by Agnes, especially on their first meeting. It's 12 p.m. when a loud buzzer sounds in the office. "What is that noise?" she asks.

"That's the boss's way of telling the natives to eat," Agnes states as she folds her fabrics into the basket on the floor. "Would you like to grab a bite with me? I could show you some nice restaurants around here."

"That's really nice of you, but I'm pretty familiar with the area. Besides, I really need to read this module so I can begin to get into the swing of things," Veronica says.

"Sure, I understand. But if you change your mind, I'll be in the diner across from the park," Agnes states.

Veronica decides to take advantage of the time on her hands and enjoy the scenery of the park next door to the building. Sitting on the bench reading her module, she pauses to admire the color scheme of the trees that the fall season has created. Another thing that catches her attention is the couples walking together hand in hand and pushing their children in strollers, which gives the park a different form of beauty. Many days she's wished for a husband and child of her own, but she knows if that's God will for her, then one day her dream will come true.

As she looks around enjoying her lunch and the lovely fall weather, she notices a familiar face passing in front of her. It is the gentleman who risked his own life to save hers from the brutal rape that Osogwa attempted that night at the club.

He is dressed nicely in business attire, holding a conversation with another gentleman. Her mind is telling her to speak, but her mouth can't seem to bring the words out to get his attention. A sudden chill comes over her body watching him pass by. She looks down to the ground in disappointment knowing this may be the only time she may ever see this man again, or at least have the chance to thank him for what he did for her. She owes her life to this stranger who saved her from the worst crime any woman could face.

Realizing that the woman on the bench is the same person who was in distress a few weeks ago, he immediately excuses himself from his conversation and heads back in her direction. He looks around in the grass, sees the last of a group of wild dandelions, and picks one up before approaching her.

"Excuse me. Do you mind if I have a seat next to you?" he asks while holding the flower.

Looking up to realize that he has returned to speak with her, she smiles and invites him to sit. The closer he moves to her on the bench, the stronger the chill grows. At one time she is so overwhelmed and nervous that she becomes a little nauseous. He hands her the flower.

"I don't know if you remember me, but I'm the gentleman from a few weeks ago who…well. I'm Keith."

"I'm Veronica. Thank you for all you did for me that night. I don't know what I would've done without you." She pauses for a moment, trying to keep herself from becoming too emotional. "You do know this flower is half dead, right?" she asks, twirling the stem between her fingers.

They both begin to laugh looking at the flower slumped over in Veronica's hand. "I know, but I figured all it needed was a little love and life would return to it before you know it," Keith says.

"Things happened so fast that night that I just lost control. I can't really explain how thankful I am, but I am. I am very, very happy that you came to my rescue," says Veronica.

"It's OK, believe me. Hey, do you like coffee? I know this great shop just two blocks from here. Maybe we can talk and catch up over a freshly brewed cup," Keith suggests.

"Actually I'm on lunch right now for a job I truly just started. If we can get it on the go, that would be great," she says.

While sitting in the café waiting to be served, they exchange small talk and discover they are both from Africa. Veronica explains how she is from a small town in Ghana, and Keith tells her he is from the inner city of Nigeria. They have both come to this country with the dreams and ambition to make it in life and support those back home. Keith explains that although he is a businessman, at times he still feels homeless and almost purposeless due to his constant traveling back and forth between the U.S. and Africa.

Veronica, obviously attracted to Keith, has just found some information that piques her curiosity. "So with you always traveling like you do, how are you able to have a social life? I mean, it definitely sounds exciting, but can you truly take care of your family this way?" she asks.

Keith sits back in his chair and smiles.

"What's so funny?" Veronica asks.

"Believe me, I'm no psychic in any way, but if you were the least bit curious I would have to say, 'No, I'm not married, nor do I have any children who would be in need of my private time,'" he responds.

"Do you really think that's what I was trying to say? I'm not that shy. Believe me, I would have just asked you. But I admit, I was a little curious," she says, blushing and smiling.

"Excuse me! Strong and confident, are we? Well, that's a beautiful quality to have as a woman," he says.

"You think so?" she asks while looking down at her watch. "Oh my! My lunch break ends in five minutes and I have to be getting back. It's my first day on the job, and I don't want to make a bad impression on the boss, you know," she says, gathering her belongings.

"Would you like me to walk you back?" Keith asks.

"No, it's fine. If I start another conversation with you, I'll definitely not make it back. You're really a nice guy," she says, looking at Keith.

"You're very nice yourself," he says. "If you need a lunch buddy or maybe want to go to dinner with a nice guy who would love to have dinner tomorrow night – his treat of course – with a nice woman by the name of Veronica, give me a call," Keith says while handing her his card.

"Sure. I'll keep that in mind. And nicely put by the way," she says.

As they stand and proceed to the door, Keith walks a few steps ahead and holds the door open. Trying not to make it too obvious, Veronica gets as close as possible to get a smell of his cologne. She is staring at the man who not only saved her life, but also is in her mind the most attractive man she has ever seen. If there is a soul mate out there for her, she hopes she's found him.

"Well, I'm going to be going this way. It was very nice seeing you again, and thanks for the coffee and conversation," she says.

"I hope it won't be the last," says Keith.

"Maybe," says Veronica before she proceeds down the block. Keith stands in front of the restaurant watching her walk, hoping she'll turn around. At that moment, Veronica turns and waves bye to him, as he gestures for her to call him with his hands.

Back in the office, Veronica is at her cubicle going over her module when she looks up and sees yet another familiar face walking across the floor. It's Linda from the coffee shop. At first she wonders what Linda is doing here, thinking to herself, *this has to be the day of coincidence if I've ever had one.* Knowing that asking Agnes who Linda is will open a can of information she doesn't really want to, she decides to keep her thoughts to herself and not become involved in other people's business. However, her curiosity gets the best of her. "Excuse me. Do you know the woman who just walked in? She really looks very familiar to me."

"Oh, that's Linda Burns, the boss' wife. From time to time she comes by just to see what's going on. A very nice lady, just totally lost to what's *really* going on. You know, I have been here for years and that man..." Agnes starts before being interrupted by Veronica.

"I'm sorry, but I was out of place for asking. She just looked like someone I met before. I didn't mean to disturb you."

"Well, excuse me!" says Agnes before turning back into her cubicle.

Meanwhile, in Mr. Burns' office, Linda stands over by the window overlooking the city skyline. "John, we really need to begin the process of getting a nanny for Zacori, especially with a new baby on the way," she says.

As Mr. Burns looks over papers at his desk, he obviously isn't paying close attention to Linda. "OK. We can get to it tonight as soon as I get – did you say a new baby?" He stands and approaches Linda by the window, wrapping his arms around her and softly kissing her on the cheek. Excited now, he repeats, "Did you say a new baby?"

"Yes, we are having a baby," she says, smiling. "I know it may seem a little soon after Zacori, but it just happened. I really wanted to tell you, but I had to make sure first. I'm sorry," Linda says.

"No, no, this is great. As a matter of fact, this is the best news I have heard since Zacori. I was the only child, and I really wouldn't want him to grow up like I did without a brother. Wow! This is great!"

"Who said it's a boy?"

"Wishful thinking. I had no idea," he says, lifting Linda up in his arms excitedly. "WE'RE HAVING A BABY!"

"That's still a long time away, but I think with this news we should really look into this nanny situation," Linda says.

"We should definitely begin looking for someone. It has to be someone very dependable and trustworthy who can do things around the house to give you a hand, especially with us expecting now," he says rubbing her belly.

"I'm not even showing yet, John. You're really excited about this, huh?"

"I am beyond words. My family is everything to me, and more than that, it's about Zacori. It would be selfish to leave him alone this world," Mr. Burns explains.

Linda wraps her arms around her husband's neck and kisses him softly on the lips. "Now, do you think we should have a live-in or someone who just comes daily? I think the best thing is someone who lives in. Once I become enormous with swollen ankles, at least you can look at another woman," she jokingly states.

"You know, that doesn't sound like a bad idea. She can walk around in a cute little maid outfit..."

"Hey! Don't get beside yourself, mister," Linda interrupts.

Mr. Burns gently guides Linda to the chocolate leather couch along the wall to sit down. "Let me worry about that. I have a lot of business associates who have nannies, and I'm sure they could recommend someone that will be great. I love you," he states, looking deeply into his wife's eyes.

"I love you too," she answers. "And before I forget, we have to start planning the company party. Are we still having it at the loft, or do you prefer the house?"

"That's four months away, dear! I know it takes a lot of work to prepare for this event, and this year I will totally leave it up to you. Just one thing: keep in mind my partners from overseas will be attending this year and I really have to impress these guys."

"That's great. Maybe this year we can have some sort of theme. How about 'Christmas in China?' We can hire some of the best chefs to make oriental cuisine. I have so many ideas; I'm super excited," she says.

"This year it is totally your show. I have total faith in you," he assures her.

"Do you think you will be home early tonight? I was thinking we could have dinner together like a normal family," Linda states sarcastically.

"I will try my best. I just have a late meeting with a business associate at 7:30 and I will be home straight after, I promise," Mr. Burns states. "I will also immediately start making calls and see who can refer a good nanny to us."

They begin to exit the office and proceed through the work area when Linda notices Veronica.

"Oh my goodness! I know her," Linda exclaims, referring to Veronica.

"Who?" Mr. Burns asks.

"The young lady sitting at the desk over there."

"Where?" he asks.

"Over there," she points. "The only woman of color in the whole office, sitting at the cubicle. I don't know if you can remember when I told you about a month ago, but I was getting coffee at the café I usually go to, and she just happened to be there. For some odd reason, Zacori was incredibly attached to her. Making a long story short, I was grabbing my coffee from the counter when it spilled on her, which stopped it from landing on Zac's face. She was so nice about it. I offered to buy her coffee as a peace offering and she refused. I have to say hello." Linda grabs Mr. Burns by the elbow and proceeds toward Veronica.

Linda waves from across the room as she approaches, while Veronica nervously waves back. She then stands to accept the hug Linda is extending.

"Oh my God! How are you? It's so good to see you," says Linda. "I'm sorry, I totally forgot your name. It begins with a V, right?"

"Yes. It's Veronica," she answers, feeling a bit awkward. She begins to adjust her hair, nervously looking toward Mr. Burns. "And how's my little friend doing?"

"He's great. I'm really sorry about what happened that day. I was just reminding my husband about the incident."

"Oh, it's OK. My hands have actually become softer since that day. Maybe I should find a way to make lotion from coffee beans," Veronica says before the two ladies briefly laugh.

"I actually had no idea of this incident until now, but I guess the two of us meeting was meant to be. And look, who would ever think that now you're a part of my business family," Mr. Burns states.

"What a coincidence. I don't mean to be rude, but I really have to get into this policy and procedure manual so I can be just as good at this job as I was at burning my hand," Veronica jokingly states in an attempt to keep things professional.

"Oh, please, continue what you were doing. Maybe I will see you again in the café since we both enjoy a great cup of coffee. I just wanted to say hello to you, and next time the coffee is on me," Linda says.

"No problem! I accept your offer. And tell my little friend I said hello," Veronica says.

"I sure will. Well, let me let you get back to what you were doing, and I'll see you later. Good to see you again," says Linda.

As the Burnses begin to walk off, Mr. Burns taps Veronica on the shoulder and gives her a slight nod. Before reaching the front door, he expresses to Linda that she must not fraternize or become too acquainted with any of the employees.

"She seems like a very nice girl, and honestly, it may sound weird, but I feel like I owe her for that day," Linda says while reaching in her purse for her keys.

Mr. Burns stands there in silence knowing the intentions that his wife has. "It is very important that we keep the relationship between management and employees professional. You are just as important and invested in this company as me, so please honey, don't become too close with the staff. Who knows, one day they may turn us against one another," he says.

"Or help us," she says, kissing him on the cheek before leaving. "Don't forget to take care of the nanny situation." Linda gives a final look to the back of the office and waves goodbye to Veronica, who returns the gesture.

As Veronica sits there, she can only think to herself *How do I get myself in these situations?* Agnes turns toward her to speak, but she holds her hand up first. "Not today, tomorrow or yesterday. I just don't want to get involved in things that may jeopardize my future."

Agnes turns back into her chair and states, "Well, excuse me again."

⌒

Later that evening, Mr. Burns arrives home, and he and his wife begin to discuss the issue of a nanny. They agree that whomever they hire has to play the roles of caretaker and maid. Linda wasn't as fortunate as he was growing up, but she always wanted the best for her children, like any parent.

"We need somebody who can cook, clean, pick up Zacori from school, help me with everyday tasks and…" Mr. Burns shakes his head as Linda talks.

"I don't mean to offend you, my dear, but slavery has been over for a long time. But I respect the fact that you want to get your money's worth." Mr. Burns begin to laugh as he states, "The next thing you're going to want her to be black and from the Caribbean."

"So what do you think that we should do? Did you speak to any of the partners you have relationships with? And what would be your issue even if I suggested that we hire a black woman to take care of our son? Please enlighten me," Linda states.

Mr. Burns stands there with his hand pressed against his chin, as if in deep thought, with a smirk upon his face. "Where should I begin? It's not that I see anything wrong with a black woman taking care of my children, but I would worry about her influence on our kids. My children will not be subjected to jungle rap music or ghetto slang. Besides, as I was taught growing up,

28

white people have the ability to structure the behavior of blacks, but blacks can never structure the behavioral patterns of whites. Why do you think the media only shows white people adopting blacks from poor countries and communities? It's how we continue to show the world our way is the best way for them, whether it's admitted or not."

Linda sits on the couch in complete shock hearing the explanation coming from her husband's mouth. "What? Wow!" she says, almost speechless at the comments he's just made. "I'm almost afraid to hear what you have to say about the success of black women or women period. But, after you continue feeding me with ignorance, please enlighten me on your theory as to what *you* think is best for our children. I would love to hear it straight from the donkey's mouth."

"Asian. I'd choose an Asian or Indian. They hold values: discipline, loyalty, obedience," states Mr. Burns while pouring a drink into his cup.

"You know what? You just do what you feel is best, Oh Great Master of All." Linda stands and immediately storms toward the bedroom, but turns around before reaching the doorway. "And by the way, I would've never thought my husband would say something so ridiculous!" She slams the door with all of her strength.

He stands by the window overlooking the city lights and proceeds to open his cell phone after taking a sip. "Hey. This is Burns. I think I will be calling in for a favor from you with one of the girls." He continues the conversation for another hour, making arrangements for the woman whom he has chosen to enter his house. There is no doubt in his mind that before going to bed, he will feel an enormous amount of tension from his wife. As he enters the bedroom, Linda remains awake, reading in bed. He sits on the edge of the bed in an effort to explain himself.

"I know that my comments were a little off the wall, but I need you to understand that I only want what I feel is best for the kids," he says. Linda, obviously aggravated, continues reading her book. Mr. Burns attempts to explain why he made the comments about minorities in his household.

"The things I said earlier may be extremely difficult for you to understand, but believe me, my reasons are valid. You see, unlike you I wasn't raised openly around other races that lived the same as my family. Most of the people of color were either house workers or just not in the immediate circle of my parents. My father practically instilled in us from kids that we should NEVER befriend minorities or incorporate our lifestyles with them."

"But this is a different time. Are those the same values you wish to instill in our son? You are a very intelligent, strong man. Don't you think it's time to break the chain of racist theories instilled in you as a child?"

"I do. But you can't change who you are overnight. I was out of line, I admit that, but all I ask is for your patience and understanding of my upbringing. Despite what I may personally feel or think, I will never raise my son or our children to hate or mistreat people in any way. I'm a work in progress, and I need your support in helping me change," he explains. "I have someone coming next week to care for Zacori whom I would like you to meet."

"How did you find someone so quickly?"

"Well, I made a few calls and luckily one of my business associates knew someone that is readily available to start," Mr. Burns says as he climbs under the covers, positioning himself snugly under Linda, who chuckles at his childlike behavior.

"I may not like the way you think about a few things, but I will support you because you're my husband. And if anything goes wrong, it's on you to fix it," she says.

Mr. Burns leans over and gently kisses his wife on the cheek before planting his head onto her belly. "I will never do anything to jeopardize the welfare of you or our children. I love you."

"I love you too," Linda replies before embracing her husband and placing her book on the night table.

Chapter 5

Four months have passed, and it seems like everything is going well for Veronica. Work has been stable, and she has been able to send home a few dollars to help her parents out. Most of all, her relationship with Keith is becoming stronger than ever. Unsure if she can call it love at this point, she uses the choice phrase "strong like." It's become a ritual for them to meet on weekends at the café to enjoy a small lunch and begin their day.

On this beautiful winter morning, large snowflakes fall to the ground shadowed by the color of Christmas lights hanging from the storefronts. Icicles form on the gutters and drops of water create sheets of ice on the ground.

"If I had to be honest, it's the snow. It's amazing to see this white substance fall from the sky and give innocence to the earth. Rain is different. It has a violent yet relaxing feel to it. The presence of lightning and thunder is incredible to me," says Keith.

Veronica begins to laugh. "You're so funny."

"Why?" he asks, laughing along with her.

"Because what do snow and violent rain have to do with why you love this country?"

"I don't know, now that I think about it. But there are definitely some great reasons why I love this country now, besides that," he says, reaching across the table and grabbing Veronica's hand. They share passionate eye contact before leaning across the table to kiss gently on the lips. He remains staring at her after they sit back in their chairs.

"What?" Veronica asks, placing her hair behind her ear and exposing her face.

"You!" he replies.

She suddenly pauses and looks toward Keith with confusion. "You know, I would have never thought in my wildest dreams that I would be here with you today. And sometimes I have to admit that I wonder why me? What is it about me that you find interesting?

"I appreciate you helping me to find myself. It's not always easy for a man, especially of my success, to find a gem in a world of trash. I do not love you for anything more than the woman you are. But there are some things that I must tell you before we go any further. Back at home…" he starts, when the bells from the entrance of the café disturb his speech. It's Linda and Zacori along with a very well groomed Asian woman approaching the counter.

"Hey! That's my boss' wife and son. If you could, just give me a minute to say hello. We sort of have a little past here," says Veronica.

"Sure, by all means," Keith responds.

As Veronica approaches Zacori, he recognizes who she is and begins to move around in his stroller with excitement. Just as excited, Veronica begins to make childish faces while bending down and tickling his belly. Zacori, turning as red as the scarf that protects his neck from the cold, buries his head into the creases of his coat. Linda stands over them shaking her head while watching the interaction between her son and his old friend. Veronica stands and hugs Linda.

"How are you? It seems like forever since we've last seen each other," asks Linda, greeting Veronica with a hug and kiss on the cheek.

"I'm great. No complaints. Things are really beginning to come together for the better."

"I see," Linda comments, all the while looking over at Keith sitting at the table reading the paper. "He's very handsome. How long have you two been married?" she asks.

"Oh, we're not married, but it is getting more-than-friends serious, if that makes sense to you. But I will tell you the story some other time," says Veronica, gesturing for Keith to come over for a more appropriate introduction. Keith approaches and extends his hand to greet Linda.

"Hi, I'm Linda. Pleasure to meet you," she says.

"And Linda this is…" Veronica begins to say before being interrupted by Keith.

"Her man! My name is Keith, and a friend of Veronica's is a friend of mine. Pleasure to meet you as well," he says.

Veronica looks at Keith in shock, though smiling at the comment that took her by surprise. "Linda, this is my man Keith, starting today or now as a matter of fact," she says. She kneels back down and continues to play with Zacori, who begins to pull on her pants leg as the adults talk.

Linda folds her arms and smiles as she witnesses the bond between the two of them. "I would be jealous if I didn't go through twelve hours of labor with him myself. This is my son, Zacori, and next to him is our nanny, Ming," she says.

The waitress approaches the counter and announces to Linda that her order is ready. Reaching into her purse, she briefly looks up and realizes that Ming's eyes are fixed on Veronica and Zacori while they play next to her.

Sensing that she is being watched, Veronica begins to feel uncomfortable with Ming standing over her staring. She looks up and asks, "Are you OK?" Linda, feeling a little tension, clears her throat to interrupt.

"I'm OK!" Ming answers and quickly begins to fix Zacori's clothes that became a little ruffled after playing with Veronica.

Veronica catches eyes with Linda and mouths, "What's going on?" while looking at Ming.

Linda shrugs her shoulders, gesturing that she has no idea. "Well, I don't mean to hold you guys up any more. Keith, it was a pleasure meeting you, and Veronica; I will catch up with you soon. Before I forget, are you coming to the company party tomorrow?" she asks.

"Is it tomorrow? I totally forgot, but I'm sure I will be there. Especially if my beautiful little friend is hosting the show," Veronica says while squeezing Zacori's cheeks.

"He may not be drinking, but he will definitely be there. Keith, maybe if you're not too busy you can escort your lovely girlfriend," states Linda.

"That's truly up to Veronica. But if she will allow me, I'm not doing anything tomorrow," Keith responds.

Feeling a little on the spot, Veronica has no choice but to agree to bring Keith along. "I see no reason why he wouldn't be there," she responds.

"That's great. Let me just write the address down for you, and we will be on our way. It takes so much to prepare for these things, you know," says Linda.

As Linda finishes writing down the address, Zacori begins to raise his arms toward Veronica to signal to her to pick him up. Ming grabs the handles of the stroller and proceeds to walk through the front door of the café. Veronica waves goodbye in a playful way as Zacori waves back bashfully. Linda, holding back her emotions but obviously annoyed with Ming's behavior, can only take a deep breath and smile as she passes the paper to Veronica before leaving.

"I don't know about you, but I think there is definitely something wrong with the nanny," says Keith.

"She's pretty scary, almost to the point that her face could be on the news for a killing spree. And speaking of, I should kill you," Veronica says, softly punching Keith in his arm.

"What did I do?" he asks, dodging her love taps.

"My man? When did we discuss that this was an official relationship?" Veronica asks.

"I knew I wanted you the day I put my life on the line to save you. I saw you in the club that night before the whole incident happened. The moment you walked in, I knew. There was no question in my mind as to where I wanted to be, and it was destiny that brought us back together today," Keith says while grabbing her hands.

"This is a little overwhelming to me. Maybe it's just going a little too fast. I really enjoy your company and I have to admit that you're a great guy, but to jump into anything more than that may just be rushing things right now," she says.

"I have not asked you for anything more than your company. I too have a lot to think about, but spending time with you only makes me realize how I truly feel."

"Fair enough, I guess," Veronica, says.

"That's it," Keith responds.

"Are you sure you would like to attend this party with me? It will only be people from work, who sometimes may not be the most social, and a few of my boss' friends. I don't know how comfortable you may be with that whole situation," she says.

"No, it's fine. If anything we will make the most of it. Your boss is a businessman like me, so it could turn out to be an opportunity, but the most important thing is being there with you." Keith looks down at his watch. "Wow! It's already two o'clock and I have a very important meeting at four. I'm afraid I have to run now. Do you need me to drop you off at home?" he asks.

"No, I think I will just sit here and finish my coffee. It's a beautiful day. Maybe I will take a nice walk and think of all that was said today," Veronica says.

Keith leans over the table and gently kisses Veronica on her cheek. "Don't think too much. I will call you a little later about meeting up tomorrow for the party," he says before exiting the café and getting into his car parked in front.

Veronica waves goodbye before seeing him pull off. Once he's out of sight, she slumps down in the chair, breathless from their conversation. "Thank you, God!" she says, looking at the ceiling and smiling.

"I agree," the cashier says from behind the counter. The two ladies share a friendly laugh before going back to what they were doing.

⁓

The next evening, Keith and Veronica arrive at the Burns' apartment on the Lower East Side. From the outside appearance, the area initially looks like a dump, but the way the city is structured, the poorest neighborhood can be right next to the richest.

"And people ask how the rich stay rich!" exclaims Keith as they walk down the dark alleyway looking for the address.

Finally arriving, they notice a large sign that reads "Fabric House Company Party in 3C," which verifies they are at the right place. After they hit the buzzer, moments later a small woman of Asian descent dressed in a Santa's helper outfit opens the cargo elevator door to meet all incoming guests. Once they enter the elevator, the bass from the music slightly rocks it.

"Wow, the music is really loud!" Veronica yells.

"Is that Prince?" Keith curiously asks.

"The Burns throw one of the best company parties of the year, so be prepared to really enjoy yourselves," the young woman states as the cargo door opens to the third floor. After walking through the hallway amazed by the Asian-influenced architecture and the immaculate condition of their surroundings, they arrive at the apartment.

"This is it. Trust me, the music is loud, but I work with these people and they can really be lame, so just smile and be as friendly as you can until it's over, no matter how hard it may seem," Veronica states before the door opens.

"Welcome to the Burns home. May I take your coat for you?" asks the hostess. "The party is located in the main room behind the sliding doors. There are numerous waitresses with drinks and eating stations throughout the loft. So without further ado, I introduce you to the Fabric House Christmas Spectacular," the young woman states while opening the doors. Immediately the aroma of food and alcohol takes over their senses.

It is standing-room only, with men dressed in business suits alongside their wives talking and exotic dancers in Santa outfits dangling from poles by the bar. Mr. Burns is singing "When Doves Cry" on a karaoke machine with his tie wrapped around his head like Rambo – obviously intoxicated and crawling on the floor.

"White people can really party!" Veronica whispers to Keith, laughing.

"They sure can," Keith responds while feeling Veronica's elbows dig into his ribs as his eyes follow the Asian women in skimpy outfits serving food and drinks. The majority of the wives in the room stand with each other almost oblivious to the activity of their husbands, who are intoxicated and careless about their behavior exhibited openly.

"If I didn't see it with my own eyes, there would be no way I could believe what is happening," Veronica says.

"This is very special, may I add to your statement? Very special!" Keith says.

After the song finishes the crowd erupts with laughter and clapping. No matter how professional these men have been in the office, they definitely know how to entertain. At this moment, Veronica begins to understand that business is not just about meetings, but trust. These men have come from all over the world to be at this party, not just for a good time, but to build trust, and if dancing off beat and crawling on the floor can make them millions of dollars, it must be fine. Keith watches along her side, just nodding his head with a smile on his face that lights up the room.

As they make their way through the crowd, Linda finally notices Veronica from across the room and begins to approach her. Greeting with a kiss on the cheek, the two ladies softly embrace one another.

"How are you? I am so happy you guys were able to make it. Thank you for coming," Linda says.

"I wouldn't have missed it for the world," states Veronica.

"Well, make yourself at home. I'm sure most of the people you may know already from work. There's food and drinks in the back, but as you notice there are a lot of young ladies walking around to serve you if needed. I have to entertain the other guests, but we will definitely be able to catch up later when things quiet down a little," says Linda before walking off.

"I'm going to walk around and say hello to some familiar faces I work with. Will you be OK for a few minutes?" Veronica asks Keith.

"Sure, I'll be fine. I have pretty good experience fitting in with businessmen. Please, go enjoy yourself," says Keith.

While admiring the paintings along the wall in the hallway, Veronica hears a strange noise she just can't ignore, as if someone is yelling in the distance. Silently walking, she approaches a door that is slightly cracked and curiously looks inside, noticing Ming holding tightly to Zacori's arm while shaking him vigorously. She taps him four times on his backside, telling him to shut up before pushing him to the bed, where he flops unable to defend himself. Veronica hits the door in an effort to stop the abuse that she is witnessing. The noise forces Ming to look up in shook, since she is clearly not expecting anyone to be in the area.

"You can't come in here. I'm trying to put the baby to sleep," Ming says, trying to put on an innocent smile.

Veronica looks at Ming suspiciously, letting her know through her facial expression that she witnessed what just occurred. She eases herself out the door and heads down the hallway to return to the party when she hears Ming violently slam the door. Entering back into the party, she notices Keith and Mr. Burns talking by the bar, but focuses mainly on looking for Linda. She wanders the room, making her way through the crowd before spotting her on the balcony.

Nervous about how to tell Linda about what she's witnessed, Veronica decides to make small talk to ease things up and get a vibe from her. "I really love what you have done with this place. The décor is beautiful, and the color scheme is breathtaking," she says.

"Thank you! It took me a long time and a lot of mistakes were made, but after countless episodes of "This Old House" and thousands of dollars in paint, I guess I did a good job, huh?" Linda responds.

"Yes, you did. I wish I'd have that problem one day: a beautiful home, a rich husband, and a live-in nanny. It must really feel good to live the life of a princess," says Veronica.

"Oh, believe me, it's not all it's cracked up to be. Having money and living the life of a person with no worries are two different things. All these men in these rooms who do business deals with my husband have their little secrets. I have been around them for years – some are good guys and some do bad business. To be rich, a sacrifice has to be made. Either it's the family or screwing over those who trust and love you," Linda replies.

Veronica remains quiet; all the while taking small sips of wine and enjoying the view with Linda on the balcony. Deep inside she knows the right thing to do is tell Linda what she saw, but over stepping her boundaries could cost her more than a friend; it could cause her to lose her job if she doesn't do things tactically. "How do you feel about your nanny, Ming? Am I saying it right?" she asks Linda.

"I have to admit she is a little weird and keeps to herself a lot. But I guess she's still adjusting. At times I see her just staring into space as if her mind is somewhere else. Have you ever felt like someone wanted to tell you something important, but was too nervous and just held it in? That's how I feel about her. Crazy, isn't it?" Linda asks.

"You can say that twice. When you guys decided to bring her on, did you ask a lot of questions? Sometimes you can really found out a lot about a person just through general conversation.

Look how we turned out – who would have thought a cup of coffee would have brought two strangers together like this?" Veronica laughs.

"To tell you the truth, I let Jim handle this one. He had his own little idea of what a good nanny would be like, so I let him run with it. Plus all his business associates are affiliated with some company that they get nannies from," says Linda.

I guess if I had a kid, one of my main concerns would be their safety. Do you feel he's safe when he is with her?" Veronica asks.

Truthfully I never really thought about it. The funny thing with nannies and hired help is, you really don't know who they are until something happens. I guess you just have faith everything will be fine. And as far as Ming, I think she's a nut, but my husband trusts her, and his business partners so; Linda says.

Veronica softly mumbles "Just a little weird," while sipping her wine.

The two friends begin to laugh as extreme laughter and horrible singing coming from the main room where the party is being held interrupt them. Curiously they look at each other before making there way back inside.

"Who in the world is that singing?" Linda asks as they approach the main room.

"I don't know, but I really wish they would stop trying," says Veronica.

As they enter the room, the image of Keith, Mr. Burns and three other men with their ties wrapped around their heads and no shirts singing "YMCA" leaves the two women standing there speechless.

"OH MY GOD!" says Veronica. Embarrassed in the moment, she folds her arms looking at Keith, who glances at her and winks before engaging in the routine again. She smiles and shakes her head, thinking she may have found the man of her dreams.

Meanwhile, Linda heads toward Zacori's room to check on him, especially considering that after her conversation with Veronica, keeping an extra eye on Ming wouldn't be a bad idea. Approaching the door, Linda eases her head to it to hear if there is any noise coming from the room first. Slightly cracking the door, she notices Ming cuddled in the bed with Zacori sound asleep in her arms. She smiles and gently closes the door.

Ming's eyes quickly open, signaling she is far from asleep.

The night has ended and the Burns are saying their final good-byes to the last guests. Veronica and Keith are two of the last to leave, assuring the couple that they'll be fine. Upon entering the cargo elevator, Keith stumbles a little bit, motioning that he probably has had one too many.

"Feeling a little bit tipsy, huh?" asks Veronica as she places her hand under his arm to catch him.

"I'll be fine. But I think it's best that we catch a cab to be on the safe side. The last thing I want to do is put my future in jeopardy because I chose not to be responsible," Keith says.

"Future?"

"Yes. You," Keith responds

Veronica catches a feeling of warmth running through her body and a weakness in places meant for adult thoughts. She cradles herself under Keith as the cargo door opens to the street. After hailing a cab from the street corner, she eases Keith into it and tells the cabbie to go uptown.

As they arrive at Veronica's house, Keith has sobered up enough to pull himself from the vehicle without any help. She can only laugh as he takes deep breaths, inhaling cold night air. Signaling for the cab to wait a few minutes, he plans to return after walking Veronica to the front door. "I had a wonderful time tonight, and I want to thank you for inviting me out with you," he says.

"It's always a pleasure to spend time with you also," she responds.

Keith firmly puts his arms around her and gently kisses her on the lips. "I will call you as soon as I get in!" he shouts, walking down the steps toward the awaiting car.

"Me or the cab?" Veronica asks.

Keith pauses and turns toward the steps smiling.

"I mean, I was just wondering if you would like to stay here and get yourself together a little bit more instead of hurrying home and falling asleep in the cab," Veronica nervously states.

"Are you sure?" he asks.

Veronica nods to assure Keith she knows exactly what she's saying.

Keith quickly goes in his pocket, nearly tearing it off to get money to pay the cab driver. "Thank you for your services, but I will not be needing you tonight. Oh yeah!" he says while trying to get his money together. "You know what? Take it all, and Merry Christmas to you and yours," he says. He throws the money into the back seat with excitement and proceeds to head to the front door, where Veronica waits, smiling.

Now in the apartment, Keith waits for Veronica as she puts on a fresh pot of coffee in the kitchen. He tries to fix himself in a sexy position, moving the pillows around and unbuttoning his shirt slightly before she returns. He checks his breath, only to notice that the aroma of alcohol remains strong as ever. He frowns, searching for something to place in his mouth, but there is nothing. Realizing that there is a rose sitting in water on the table, he hesitates for a minute before plucking a petal off and quickly chewing it. Veronica places a fresh cup of coffee in front of him and sits down on the couch. Keith, still with the rose petal in his mouth trying to remain cool, is hesitant to drink the coffee. Veronica looks over realizing there are rose petals on the table and begins to giggle once she realizes what Keith may have done.

"FYI, I always keep some form of candy in the little draw under the table," she says while blowing into her cup.

Keith slowly opens his mouth and pushes the rose petal into a napkin as they both begin to laugh. "What is so funny?" he asks.

"Besides you eating a rose petal in my living room, it's the image of you and my boss singing 'YMCA' with two Chinese men with no shirts on, rocking back and forth. It's one of the funniest things I have ever seen!" Veronica says, hysterically laughing at this point.

"I am glad you enjoyed the view," Keith states as he begins to join the laughter.

"But you want to know what I enjoyed most of all?" she asks.

"What was that?"

"Watching you walk around a room full of strangers confidently networking and eventually gaining enough trust to actually have them join you in a karaoke performance. All I was thinking was, *Look at this strong, confident black man – my man – working it.* It made me feel so amazing," she says.

Keith looks at Veronica before moving closer to her on the couch.

She takes his hand and slowly glides it down to her side, allowing him to feel the curves she is blessed to have. She escorts him to the bedroom, where a candle allows just enough light for them to see their silhouettes in the background. The aroma of sweet-smelling wax adds to the sense of seduction as they passionately kiss.

"Wait! I don't know exactly what this is or where it's going. But I have to ask you, if I'm correct about what I'm feeling right now, are you ready?" he asks.

"Do you believe a person can fall in love too soon?"

"That's something I can't answer, only because I've already become the victim of the very thing you asked about," Keith responds.

Veronica places her hands upon his chest and looks toward the floor.

"Did I say something wrong?" Keith asks.

"No! I just realized that making the right decision with my body is just as important to you. I don't know if I'm ready, but I don't want to make a mistake and risk losing you," Veronica says as tears begin to slowly drip from her eyes.

"Then we will wait. And when you're ready, I'll be lying right here next to you, waiting for you to receive me with an open heart and mind. I do not want to enjoy your body when it's your soul I need," Keith says. He gently kisses the palm of her hand as they glide down the bed staring into each other's eyes.

Chapter 6

After a few weeks of really observing Ming following the party, Linda has grown more suspicious of her behavior with Zacori. Sitting in the kitchen with Mr. Burns, Linda feels it's the best opportunity to finally discuss her concerns while he sits and reads the paper.

"There is something I really need to talk to you about, and I need your undivided attention," she says.

"Sure, honey. What's on your mind?" Mr. Burns replies as he folds the paper to listen.

"How much exactly do we know about Ming? I mean, I always thought her behavior was a little different, but I think there's something going on with Zacori," she says.

Mr. Burns sits silently in his chair and becomes interested in his wife's concerns. He may always be occupied with work, but deep in his heart he knows if anything were to happen with his son, there would be no one else to blame but himself.

"What makes you believe something is going on with our son and Ming?" he asks.

"I decided to spend more quality time with him and do the motherly things that Ming would usually handle. As I was giving him a bath yesterday, I couldn't help but to notice that there were some peculiar marks on his lower back and behind. I'm not insinuating that she is abusing him, but I am curious as to why his behavior around her is abnormal, nervous almost. And I believe before we go ahead and start blaming anyone, we should find out the facts," Linda says.

"Let's be clear on what you're saying. Are you telling me that you believe our nanny is abusing our son?" he asks.

"What I'm saying is her behavior is very suspicious and our son has marks that I've never seen before on his backside. As your wife and his mother, I need your support in this to find out the truth," Linda explains.

"Those are some serious accusations, Linda. She has been here for only a few months and was recommended by some very close business partners of mine. Are you sure that you're not overreacting, or your hormones are going a little crazy?"

Linda slams the dish on the table in front of her. "How dare you? How dare you sit there and say something as evil and ignorant to me, you self-centered jerk? It was I who carried our child for nine months with back pain and swollen feet, not some slanted-eyed psycho you hired. It doesn't matter how many nannies or servants your money can buy; I am his mother and that's the bottom line," she says furiously before heading over to the window to look at the gray city sky.

Realizing that his response was totally inappropriate, he approaches Linda by the window and wraps his arms around her. "Excuse me for my ignorance," he says, lowering his hands over her belly. There will never be anyone in this world that could take the place of you. What I said was totally wrong and stupid, and I ask that you forgive me for this. If you truly feel that something is wrong, then I will back you one hundred percent, but tell me what your plan is. Do you have a plan?" he asks.

"Let's record her every move when we are not home," Linda suggests.

"And how do you expect us to do that?" Mr. Burns asks.

"I was thinking we can have someone install cameras in the house on her day off, and maybe a nanny camera in his stroller to record when he is with her outside. I don't know, maybe I have been watching too much television, but I have a gut feeling something is wrong," she says.

"I don't think following her around during the day when she is not with Zacori is wise; that's invading her privacy. But I will agree to put surveillance cameras in the house. Let me ask you a question: what will happen if we find out or see things that may seem odd to you? I met this young lady – excuse me, she was referred to me by some of my closest clients. If we accuse her and are wrong, it may affect relationships with some of my overseas business partners," he says.

"So! I don't care. This is our son," Linda says while looking Mr. Burns in the eyes.

"Fine, you're right. Tomorrow, we'll give her the day off and start making the arrangements for the cameras to be installed throughout the house. I'm hoping for the best, for our family's sake," Mr. Burns says.

"I feel the same way – believe me I do," Linda says.

⟨⟩

On the other side of town, sitting in his office with his longtime friend and business partner is Keith looking over some last minute paperwork. Things have not been going so well financially for the company since the 9/11 attacks on New York City, not to add that they are two black men trying to compete with major American corporations over airline freight.

"It's going to be very difficult for us to survive the next quarter with our partners in London, especially with the price of imports at this time," the partner explains.

"So what do you suggest we do?" Keith asks.

"I don't know, to be honest with you. As I was going over the numbers last night, I found the only way we can survive is by decreasing import costs, and though this may sound terrible, a 10 percent decrease in staff may help," his partner explains.

"I can't. I won't cut any of the factory workers' jobs or salaries. They're the backbone of this company, not to mention the majority of our workers have families and some of the female employees are single mothers. We can't. There has to be another way," Keith says.

"There is no other way. You worry about their families, but what about ours? Let's be realistic here. There is no organized union here to intervene if jobs are cut or layoffs take place. We have done this before to save our asses. It's not personal, my good friend. It's business."

"I am not in disagreement with you on the nature and importance of your suggestion, but it's the disturbance or destruction of other people's livelihoods that I am against," Keith explains.

The partner leans into his chair before thrusting his pen onto the financial books in front of him. He glances at Keith before he begins to deviously chuckle. Keith can only look at his longtime friend and partner, who strikes a cigar.

"What is so funny? This is very serious matter we are dealing with right now," Keith asks.

"I see what's going on, my good friend. It is the girl."

"What girl? I have no idea what you're speaking of," Keith responds.

"Oh, you know exactly what I am talking about. You have grown feelings for the factory girl," his partner says while laughing.

"She has nothing to do with the decisions I make for my company, nor does she influence the way I feel," says Keith.

"You never cared about the feelings of those who were socially beneath you until you fell in love with someone who is. My poor brother," the partner says, blowing smoke into the air as he laughs and nods his head.

Keith's face fills with rage as he looks at his partner. He remains speechless for a moment as he gathers his thoughts about the reality of a harsh truth. "That's absolutely ridiculous. Veronica is totally different from those I employ. She is my partner, not my employee," he says.

"Different? She is a factory worker, my friend, in a relationship with a possible future Fortune 500 CEO. My words may seem harsh, but she is beneath you. She is the very…"

"ENOUGH!" Keith yells, slamming his hand on the table and causing papers to fly onto the floor. "How dare you sit there and disrespect the woman in my life? You, of all people, have no authority to judge. How soon money makes us forget that from which we came. Your wife is the daughter of a coal miner and is as educated as a whore who walks the streets of our motherland infecting men with HIV and killing our youth off slowly. How dare you, you peasant! Remember this: I started this company and brought you in, not the other way around," Keith says.

The room remains silent, as the two friends sit saying nothing. Keith's partner continues to smoke his cigar while Keith hangs his head and clutches his hands.

"I hope you are not speaking of all my wives, because that just may have hurt my feelings," the partner says before the two men can no longer hold in their laughter. "Keith, I never meant to disrespect you or her. It's just that we have a lot to lose, brother, and I hope you understand that," he says.

"I know you meant no harm, and you know no matter what, we will always remain brothers. From the country to here! Never will money or women come between what we worked so hard for," says Keith.

"On a serious note, how do you feel about her? Is it wedding-bell feelings or a simple fling that will soon come to an end?" his partner asks.

Keith pauses for a moment. "It's almost something that I can't explain in words. She's special in her own way. She has her own style and way of doing things. I have been with a lot of women in my life, but she's different. I feel complete when I'm around her," Keith explains.

"Wow, that was a serious Oprah moment. I have never heard you speak of a woman like that. But as your friend I have to ask you something. Have you told her about the wives back home and the children? And will she be willing to accept her role in an Islamic household and culture once you convert over?"

Keith sits back in his chair, bringing his hands above his head and taking a deep breath. "That's something I can only explain in due time. First I must go to Ghana and learn who the parents are, receive the blessings of the father. I have to do things traditionally to truly bring this together," he says.

"I believe so, but one thing you must do is be honest. If you truly love her as you say, then you should have told her of the things that are important to you back home. This is a culture of different values and beliefs so don't be surprised, brother, if she will not accept the religion or traditional ways of our lifestyle. She may be from Ghana – that's fine, but she is not Muslim," his partner explains.

"I understand, but my feelings tell me to keep this a secret until we are solid on where we are going as a couple. First I will travel home to get the acceptance of the elders, and then ask for her hand. I shall visit her home and shower them with gifts to assure them that she is in good hands with me. I have a lot to explain, but I know that she loves me as I love her," Keith says.

"Whatever it is you decide to do in life, I shall support you, brother. All I need to have explained to me is how in the world you are going to explain to a single woman in the U.S. that you have three wives and six kids at home," his partner says, hysterically laughing.

"I have no idea!" Keith responds, letting out a stressed sigh before leaning back in the chair and looking at the sky. While his partner remains laughing, Keith tosses the papers that were on the desk at him.

"I know the number of a great urologist downtown who will help you with all your future trouble," his partner says.

The two gentlemen share a good laugh and tap their glasses as a toast to the future.

Chapter 7

Linda and Veronica have begun spending more time with one another and formed a pretty strong friendship despite the wishes of Mr. Burns. Today is a beautiful day. The trees are full of birds singing, and the flowers give life to the grass that lay dead all winter. The sound of children laughing and local musicians playing on park benches is evidence that the streets of New York are back to life. Linda is going on her fourth month of pregnancy, and all is well with Keith and Veronica. With both of the men in their lives always traveling for business reasons, they have a lot of free time to enjoy each other's company. Veronica has learned through Linda that it's just part of being with a successful man.

The ladies need each other and depend on one another. They get each other through lonely nights and afternoon coffee binges when Mr. Burns is away on business. Veronica usually keeps her feelings about Ming, who still displays weird behavior, to herself, and she has so much fun with Linda, it's as if Ming isn't even there. Linda is glowing during pregnancy, and Veronica is living the experience vicariously through her. It seems nothing can get in the way of the bond they share. They are alone for long periods of time, and it is good for the both of them to have someone to talk to, free from the normal activities of their lives. Veronica experiences the life of a rich woman with children, and Linda experiences what it's like to be single and free again, away from the snobs who are married to the other board members in the firm. Veronica gives her youth and joy.

Little does anyone know that Linda is the total opposite of what they all perceive her to be. She was once very poor and moved to New York with dreams of being a dancer before meeting Mr. Burns while working as a receptionist.

"When I first came to this city, believe it or not, I was just like you. I wanted to explore the arts and fulfill my dreams of becoming a dancer on Broadway," Linda says.

"Really? So what happened?" Veronica asks.

"Well, one day this charming young man walked into where I was working, looking for directions to the main office. We got into a conversation, which at the time was probably one of the weirdest I'd ever had with a man, but somehow it was the sweetest and most innocent exchange of words I've ever had. Needless to say, time went by and we started dating. Next thing I knew, I was married and planning on having a child," Linda says.

"I would have never thought that you were not born into wealth. I thought you were accustomed to being knee-deep in it," Veronica states.

"Yeah, I was knee-deep all right – in tuna fish with wheat bread every night. He saved my life, just like Keith will one day save yours. We are the lucky ones, sister," Linda says while grasping Veronica's hand.

"I guess we are, huh?" she responds. Looking around in the park, Veronica can't help but to realize the vast majority of women of color sitting with Caucasian children. She guesses that these women are nannies, most of them from the West Indies or Africa due to their features. She sits, quietly amazed at how the children run to the nannies for love and comfort while the mothers sit talking on their cell phones as if they aren't even there. The more she looks around, the more her eyes open up to the reality of what she might be facing.

"Are you OK? You have been sitting there quiet while I have been running my mouth off. What's on your mind?" Linda asks.

"Oh, nothing. I was sitting here looking around, and it amazes me how many black women are here in the park with white kids, and the kids are just so attached to them. It's like they have taken the place of the mothers who are right there next to them," Veronica says.

Linda pauses for a moment to observe what Veronica is speaking about. "Wow, you're right! I guess I never paid attention to it until now," she says.

For a short while, the two ladies gaze at the amount of women in the park watching over and nurturing children who are not of their own loins. Veronica periodically glances over at Linda, who seems just sat amazed.

"You know, when we were looking for a nanny, my husband probably had the same mentality of most of the people in this park. I'm almost ashamed to say it, but he insisted that we not hire a woman of color and referred to these terrible stereotypes that were embedded in his head as a child" Linda says.

"Really? I wouldn't have sensed that from Mr. Burns. He always seemed like such a kind, sweet man, never someone who held racist thoughts," Veronica responds.

"You never know. Look at all these people. Do you think they hired someone of color with the intentions of giving them a job, or is the mental image of 'Big Mama' somewhere hidden in their minds? It's the same theory of that old slave woman raising the white young, only to have to deal with inadvertent racism from the same child later on in life," Linda says.

"I think we should change the subject; it's beginning to feel a little awkward now. You know, I always wanted to ask you, what is it like being married and having children, just being happy?" Veronica asks. Linda begins to laugh. "What's so funny?"

"I have never met anyone who was happily married yet, to answer that," Linda responds. The ladies begin to laugh as Linda touches her belly. "I see someone agrees with me."

The ladies notice Ming coming slowly from the distance, with Zacori slumped over in his stroller, obviously unhappy about something that took place during with his time alone with her. As Ming approaches, Linda looks at Zacori and realizes something is definitely wrong at this point. His face seems as if he's too petrified to move or make a sound.

"Will you look at this? I can't wait until tonight to see the truth," Linda thinks to herself.

"I don't get her, Linda. I am sorry – I don't mean to be in your business, but there is definitely something wrong with this picture and her," Veronica says.

"Don't worry. Ever since we spoke at the company party, I have kept a closer eye on her. I really haven't found anything concrete as of yet, but we have to meet with an investigator today because he feels there is something he's observed he wants us to take a look at. After tonight, I'll definitely know what this bitch has been up to," Linda states.

"If you need me for anything, please don't hesitate to call me. You may be pregnant, but I'm not," Veronica says just before Ming arrives. She then reaches down into the stroller and swings little Zacori around in the air. He begins to smile and joyfully chuckle, seemingly comforted in Veronica's arms.

"You are so cute," she says, kissing him on his cheeks before giving him to Linda.

Ming suddenly grabs him and begins to fix his clothes. Veronica pauses for a moment and stares into her eyes. "So how are you today?" she asks.

Ming only nods her head submissively.

"OK … well, Linda, I have to go sweetie. Give Mr. Burns my love and remember, if there is anything you need from me tonight, don't hesitate to call me," Veronica says while gesturing to Linda that she is ready for a fight by placing her fist in the palm of her hand.

Linda smiles with amusement. "No problem. I will call you a little later if anything," she says.

They depart with a loving hug, which Veronica puts a little more strength into to let Linda know that she is there for her.

"Don't forget. I will be waiting by the phone until I hear your voice. Goodbye, my little Zacori," Veronica says. She waves goodbye while observing Linda and Zacori walking away, with Ming slowly following behind them. *What a weirdo*, she says to herself, thinking of Ming's behavior. Her phone rings suddenly, and she reaches deep into her purse to retrieve it.

"Hello? Oh, hi, sweetie," she says realizing it's Keith on the other end.

"Hello, my dear! What are you up to?" he asks.

"Oh, nothing. Just finished meeting with Linda in the park, talking and hanging out. How about you? Are we still having dinner tonight?" she asks.

"I'm sorry; that's why I am calling you. I have been called into an emergency meeting with some business partners in Africa that has forced me to leave right away. I am actually in the airport at this moment," he says.

"So when will you return?" she asks.

"I am not sure. This may take me a good while, maybe a month. I am sorry to be telling you at the last minute, but I hope you understand. I will make it up to you in 500 ways when I return," he says.

"Well, you haven't really left me a choice, but I understand you have to do what you have to do. I wish you a safe flight, and call me when you get there," Veronica says.

"Are you going to miss me?" Keith asks.

"No!" she jokingly responds.

"Really? Well, I'm going to miss you every step of the way. And Veronica – I love you," he says.

"I … love you too," she responds, hesitating for a moment before they simultaneously end the call. Still in shock after realizing how she is truly beginning to feel about Keith and knowing that he feels the same way, she sits on the bench watching the sun rays provide a mirage of gold on the waves of the Hudson River.

Later that evening, the Burns sit with the investigator to review the tapes from the surveillance cameras placed strategically throughout the house. "Are you sure you are ready to view what took place in your home?" he asks while preparing the tapes.

The Burns look at each other nervously and nod their heads yes. Linda clutches her hands together to prepare herself for the unknown. It is in this moment that the reality of her son possibly being abused by a woman her husband brought into her house sets in. Unable to hold back the tears, she gently wipes her eyes on the sleeve of her sweater. Mr. Burns continually adjusts himself in his seat, feeling a little uncomfortable as he prepares for the worst.

"I must admit we found some things that can be a little disturbing about your nanny's behavior toward your son," the inspector comments.

The Burnses sit together watching the abuse their son has suffered on different occasions. The way he handles the forceful blows to his head and body shows that he has become accustomed to the beatings.

"Oh my God! Oh my God!" Linda says while sliding to her knees, hopelessly looking at the tape. The room remains silent except for her moans as she clutches her stomach on the floor. Mr. Burns feels pain also, but knows that his cannot compare to the cries of his wife. Knowing that this is more his fault than anybody's as the person responsible for bringing this woman into their house, he launches the vase sitting on the table at the wall.

"DAMN IT!" he yells.

"You brought this monster into our house, around our son, John! How could you? How could you?" Linda pleads, desperately searching for answers.

"I'm sorry. I am so sorry!" Mr. Burns says, wiping the tears from his eyes. "I will fix this baby. I promise you I will fix this if it's the last thing I do on this earth. What do we do now?" he asks the investigator.

"The only suggestion I can make, sir, is to immediately alert the authorities and use this tape as evidence to prosecute your nanny on child abuse and endangering the welfare of a child. It seems like a pretty open-and-shut case. I have a few friends in the district attorney's office I can call to speed up the process. Of course, with your permission," he says.

"Absolutely! I want to press full charges against her," Mr. Burns insists.

"The first thing we need is an address where she can be found when she's not here," says the investigator.

Mr. Burns immediately grabs a piece of paper from the table and begins to write down where she can be found. 342 East 86th Street is the address he hands to the investigator, who briefly looks up at him as he consoles Linda, obviously distraught by what she just witnessed.

"That's all we need, along with the proof from this tape, to obtain a warrant. I have to ask you, before we begin the process to prosecute her, is there anything that we should know that may intervene with our investigation?" the investigator asks.

"I don't understand. What do you mean?" Linda asks.

"What I'm asking is how did you meet her? What was the hiring process, and who recommended that she work for you?"

"She was recommended by some of my business associates who already have nannies from the agency she works for. I assumed it was a good idea at the time, but after what we just saw, I'm lost for words," Mr. Burns says while placing his arms around his distraught wife.

"I will make some phone calls and get back in touch with you by tomorrow, after I speak to my detective friends. Until then, Mr. and Mrs. Burns, try to relax," the investigator states before shaking Mr. Burns' hand and exiting the room.

Linda sits in the chair, emotionless with a dark blank stare in her eyes. Feeling Mr. Burns' hands touching her shoulders, she immediately turns and slaps him on the side of his face. "How dare you bring that animal to our son? In the home we built to protect and love him?" she asks.

"I'm so sorry! I am so sorry," he pleads. "I will fix this, I promise."

"No! No! This isn't happening," she screams before desperately falling to her knees.

Together they sit on the floor consoling one another after realizing the mistake they made. The look on Mr. Burns' face is one of confusion and anger, but his major concern is the business relationship between him and his partners. Knowing he can't even dare to go against or say anything to stop the process of prosecuting Ming or his marriage will be over, Mr. Burns sits with his wife afraid of what the future may hold.

It's nine o'clock, and Ming is in her apartment as she usually is at night, when she hears a knock on the door. Not accustomed to having company, she ignores the knocks at first, assuming someone has the wrong apartment. After the third set of knocks increases in volume, she decides to answer the door. Slowly she walks and looks through the peephole, vaguely seeing three people whose faces she can't identify.

"How may I help you?" she asks.

"My name is Mr. Wilson, and this is detective Stacy McLaughlin from the 23rd precinct. We would love if you could open the door so we can ask you a few questions," says the investigator.

"Why are you here? You must have the wrong apartment," she replies.

Detective McLaughlin bangs on the door. "Listen! We are here to question you about a situation that occurred at the Burns house a few days ago involving you and their child. Now if I were you, I would cooperate and open the door to make things easy. We already have a warrant for your arrest; so open the door or we will open it for you. NOW!"

Ming slowly opens the door, looking through the crack and exposing her face before being pushed inside by the uniformed officer. Mr. Wilson hands her the warrant while Detective McLaughlin begins to read her rights. Though she has not been in the country for a long time, the seriousness of the officers' actions gives her the feeling that things are not good. After the detective searches her and places her hands behind her back to put on the handcuffs, Ming can only ask, "What have I done? What have I done?"

She is taken from her apartment and escorted to the police car, where she is placed in the back. Ming stares out of the window as the car begins to drive down the street, focusing directly on the female detective with a look of despair. The detective is talking to another officer, but notices the desperate stare that Ming has given her.

Once in the precinct, Ming is moved into the interrogation room, where she stares at the dark gray walls with a video camera on the edge of the table pointed in her direction. From watching television shows, she knows behind the mirror on the wall in front of her is a bunch of people waiting to listen to her every word. Due to the language barrier, the court has decided it is best to appoint her a Cantonese-speaking lawyer.

The court-appointed lawyer, Detective McLaughlin and the investigator enter the room and take seats at the table. Initially relieved to see someone with features similar to her own, she also knows that in America, things are not always what they seem. The ladies, both holding folders in one hand and coffee in the next, sit on either side of Ming, who remains silent and only glances at the women.

"Hello. My name is Tracy Xing, and I was sent by the court to represent and help you all I can. First, I must ask, do you understand the charges brought against you?"

"No!" Ming says, staring straight ahead at the wall.

"Let me assist you with this. The charges that you are facing include endangering the welfare of a child and neglect. If cooperation is not your main objective, you will be on Rikers Island in a moment," the detective says.

As the lawyer translates exactly what the detective has said, Ming remains emotionless as she stares at the desk. "Ming, you must understand the accusations that have been brought against you. They will put you in a cage as if you were a monster. You have to tell us exactly what happened," she pleads.

"Don't waste your breath. She knows what she did. I bet you there's not one bone in her body with regrets," the detective says while staring into Ming's eyes. "Do you have any idea of the pain and torture you put that innocent boy through?" Answer me! Do you?" she screams.

The lawyer begins to interpret when Ming suddenly stops her. "Do you have any idea what I have been through?" she mumbles.

Silence fills the room after Ming speaks and tears slowly begin to trickle down her cheek. The ladies anticipate her next words, but nothing comes. The detective and lawyer look at each other. As bad as the detective wants to push Ming's buttons for information, she knows the best way is to remain silent and allow Ming the time she needs.

"Ming, I know you have been through some things, but the only way we can help you is for us to understand you," her lawyer says calmly while handing her a glass of water. The detective hands her a box of Kleenex.

"There are certain things I can never say to you of my past, but I am no monster. If you really need to know, it is Mr. Burns and his associates who are the real monsters. You can't even imagine the things those gentlemen are into," she says while placing her hands in her lap.

"What exactly does that mean?" the attorney asks.

"It means he owns me," Ming whispers.

"You don't work for him anymore, Ming. You don't have to be submissive to protect anyone. I need you to understand that accusations made can put you in prison for a long time," the lawyer states.

"You really have no idea, do you? I am not his employee. I am his property through purchase," Ming says, looking angrily at the wall.

The lawyer excuses herself and leaves the room with the detective to speak outside. She explains to the detective that many women, especially of Asian descent, are sometimes forced into prostitution by rich businessmen pretending to help them find better lives, and she can almost guarantee that this is Ming's story.

"How are we ever going to get her to admit that?" the detective asks.

"By offering her freedom!"

The detective bursts into laughter. "Do you really expect me to believe that a rich businessman – excuse me – a rich, *married* and successful businessman who has ties all over the world, has put his wife and child in danger by moving his purchased sex slave into his home, leading to the abuse of his only son?"

"Yes! So I suggest you kindly give the DA a call and begin re-evaluating exactly what could have happened here. I would also like to meet with my client alone, before there is any more questioning. If what she is saying is true, we may have discovered the link to a sex trade operation right here in New York City," the lawyer says.

The detective reaches to her hip and grabs her cell phone to make the call.

⌐

Meanwhile, Veronica is in her apartment reading, as she usually does when she has time alone to relax. Comfortable on the couch, she's hesitant to answer the ringing phone until she looks over to the caller ID and realizes it's her parents.

"Hello? Oh, hi Mommy," she says.

"Veronica how is everything?" Mom asks.

"All is well. Is something wrong? It's not usual for you to call me on a Saturday. I expected you to be in church by now."

"Usually I would be, but we had an unexpected visitor and decided to enjoy this morning with breakfast at home. I must admit, you're really lucky to have a man in your life that is so caring and into you."

Veronica pauses for a moment in an attempt to understand her mom's statement and places her book on the table. "What man, Mommy?" she curiously asks.

"Keith! He says that he is your boyfriend and things have become very serious. He has come with gifts and a good heart to ask your father and myself for your hand in marriage, and discuss the plans he has for you and the family you will have," Mom says.

"WHAT?" Veronica aggressively asks. "Where is he? Put him on the phone, now!" she screams.

"Hush your tone when speaking to me!" Mom responds. "Now it seems by your reaction that you knew nothing of his being here, but there is no need to be harsh. You should embrace the fact that you have found a man who still knows the purpose of family values and respect and would do things to honor his name as he sees fit. In a lot of ways I see your father in him," says Mom.

"Sorry, Mom! But I can't believe that he would do such a thing without talking to me first or seeing if I was on the same page with him. And how did he even know where to find you guys?"

"He is in love, my child, and when a person is truly in love they can move mountains in order to make a path to happiness. Do not condemn him for following his heart, but embrace the reality of him having one. Now I must go. He and your father will return soon and I must prepare dinner for them before Keith leaves. But you must promise me that this will stay between us and you will not speak of what I told you," her mother says.

"I promise. I love you, Mom."

"And I love you, my child. Take care of yourself. Bye!" Mom says before hanging up the phone.

Afterward, Veronica sits silently on the couch in deep thought about everything that has just happened. Even though she realizes the lengths that Keith has gone through to show his love for her, she still cannot help but to feel he's violated her privacy. *I must really be American now*, she thinks to herself, knowing at home this is how things are traditionally done. Smiling like a child thinking of someone doing something so extreme for her, she feels warmth overcome her body. "He really loves me," she repeats to herself.

Chapter 8

As the workweek begins, all seems typical for the ladies working in their cubicles. Agnes remains complaining and gossiping about the ladies without green cards being overpaid and the rest of the workers are just routinely fulfilling their assignments. It isn't unusual to see Linda come in with little Zacori dangling from the side of the stroller sleeping, but what's different today is that Linda is pushing the stroller and there is no Ming humbly following behind. Instead there are two ladies giving off an air of authority followed by two uniformed officers. It seems strange to Veronica, but she dares not ask.

Linda comes over to her cubicle to briefly say hello and embrace her with a hug like she usually does when in the office. The look of worry on Linda's face and her urgency to leave make Veronica ask questions. "Is everything OK, Linda? You seem worried about something."

"I guess maybe I'm just tired. I will call you later to fill you in, but I have to go to the office right now. Do you mind just keeping an eye on Zacori for a few minutes while I speak to my husband and these other people? It is really important."

"OK, that's no problem. Take your time. We'll be right here," Veronica assures her.

"I really appreciate you just keeping Zacori busy," Linda says before walking rapidly to her husband's office. Moments later, four uniformed officers arrive at the receptionist's desk looking for the detective and private investigator. It seems as if the whole factory has stopped working for the time being, with everyone staring at the uniformed officers walking quickly from the main floor toward the offices. Obviously they need to be directed on where to go exactly, but it doesn't look good at this point. Some people think they are the INS, so Agnes tells them that every few years the immigration service does a sweep and takes half of the work force away. Most of the office appears to be sneaking out the back door.

"What in the world is going on in here today?" says Veronica.

"God bless America, our home sweet home! God bless America, our home sweet home," Agnes sings. As she stands in the walkway singing with her hand rested over her heart and a smile on her face, the officers enter Mr. Burns' office. Veronica begins to loosen the buttons on Zacori's jacket as a distraction from all the commotion. As she glances up toward the office, Mr. Burns' hand gestures are an indication that somebody is in trouble. Meanwhile, the Burns are questioning the police presence in their building.

"Someone has a lot of explaining to do about why all this commotion has entered my place of business!" What is this about?" Mr. Burns asks angrily.

"Sir, I am going to have to ask you to have a seat while we explain why we are here today," the investigator suggests.

Mr. Burns turns to his bar and fixes himself a stiff drink before returning to the couch where Linda nervously sits. She extends her hand to him as he sits loosening his tie. "Somebody better start talking soon. All I have heard so far is garbage!" Mr. Burns screams.

"Please, explain why we are here." Linda asks.

"Mr. and Mrs. Burns, during our questioning of Ming, she made some very peculiar statements in relation to how she and your husband actually met and the nature of their relationship," says the detective.

"Which leads us to believe that she may have had a personal motive that led to the abuse of your son," the investigator states.

Linda looks at Mr. Burns, who at the moment sits silent in his chair with concern on his face. "I don't understand. Ming was recommended to us by some of our closest friends who also have nannies," she says.

"That may be true, but unfortunately we have reason to believe differently, Mrs. Burns. According to Ming, she and Mr. Burns met under totally different circumstances quite a long time ago in Japan while he was on a business trip, and they..."

"That's enough!" Mr. Burns interrupts. "I think it's time for me to call my lawyer." He turns to Linda. "Honey, don't say another word!" he demands.

"No, I think I want to hear this," says Linda. "Please! Tell me what Ming has said about the relationship between her and my husband," she asks.

"I said this is the end of this foolishness, NOW!" Mr. Burns yells.

"And I said I want to hear this. Not from you or anyone else but the investigator at this time," Linda calmly responds. "Please proceed with what she has told you."

"According to Ming, she was indeed first introduced to your husband by some business associates of his in Japan, but not as a nanny. You see, Ming is one of thousands of women who are bought and sold every day to rich or even crime-related men like your husband. They are basically slaves to these men until their debt is paid or they're released from prostitution," the investigator explains.

"Prostitution?" Linda asks.

"Indeed. In fact, as per Ming, YOU, Mr. Burns, have had a long-standing relationship with Ming through this illegal act, which leaves me no choice but to place you and your wife under arrest for soliciting prostitution, human trafficking and harboring illegal immigrants on U.S. territory. Can you please stand?" he says.

"This is ridiculous! I want to speak to my lawyer immediately!" shouts Mr. Burns.

As the officers walk toward Mr. Burns to place the cuffs on him, he resists, trying to avoid being handcuffed. Forcefully the officers place him on the ground, causing a loud thump.

"What do you think is going on up there?" Veronica asks as she holds Zacori in her arms.

As Mr. Burns is being escorted to the main entrance in cuffs, a female officer reaches over to Linda and gently lifts her off the couch before placing her hands behind her back. "This is ridiculous – I didn't do anything!" she frantically screams at the officer. I have done nothing wrong. Please, I am seven months pregnant. Please don't take me away. I have a son. Somebody do something," she pleads, but it is obviously too late.

The officers begin to escort the Burnses through the corridor of their well-established business in handcuffs while whispers fill the room. Linda looks at Veronica, who is shielding Zacori's face into her shoulder to hide him from the commotion. Overwhelmed by what is going on, Veronica can't help but to cover her mouth in shock with her eyes filling with tears as she watches her friend helpless in custody.

"Take Zacori with you! I will call you as soon as I can," Linda yells across the room.

The workers have planted their faces against the front windows, watching their boss being escorted into the back seat of an awaiting squad car.

"Back to work! Back to work!" The VP shouts.

Veronica begins to realize she has the responsibility of a child on her hands. She looks down at him and smiles while gently blowing air. *I have watched kids before but never overnight. What am I supposed to do to feed him or even bathe him*, she thinks to herself while watching Zacori on the floor playing with the small car Linda left in the stroller.

It's five o'clock and the workday has finally come to an end. The buzz around the office is asking if there will even be a job to come to tomorrow with the Burnses being taken to jail. Veronica has no time to worry about tomorrow; she can only be concerned about tonight and what to do with Zacori. She gathers her things and places Zacori in the stroller as Agnes approaches.

"Do you think you will be OK? " asks Agnes.

"You know, the funny thing is that all I can actually think about is what I am going to feed him. I'm sure I will be fine. How hard can this actually be?" Veronica says smiling.

"If you need any help, don't hesitate to give me a call. But you're a smart kid, and your people are good at things like this," Agnes says before walking off.

Veronica shakes her head, ignoring the ignorant statement from Agnes while gathering Zacori's belongings.

Later, Veronica arrives at the supermarket with Zacori, trying to figure out exactly what she will have to do for the evening. She can't help but to worry about her poor friend Linda, and how she's dealing with her situation. It makes her think of Keith for a moment and how a relationship with a rich man could be. *I guess in life sometimes a sacrifice has to be made by all women*, she thinks to while approaching the line to pay for her food. She suddenly realizes how so many people are smiling and commenting positively to her as she walks around with Zacori. She overhears comments like "How cute" and other parents telling their children, "Look at the cute little boy." It makes her feel a little special, having a child with her and getting a different kind of attention.

Once at home, Veronica prepares a meal, which only consists of finger foods and ravioli. Zacori looks as he though he is enjoying it before the phone rings. Racing to the phone, she rushes to pick up the call, hoping its Linda to give her some information about what happened.

"Hello, Linda?" she asks.

"Yes, it's me," Linda replies.

"Oh my God, how are you? Is everything OK? Are you OK?" Veronica sincerely asks.

"Yes, I am fine. I don't really know what is truly going on yet, but I can say that I am fine. How is Zacori?"

"He is here with me doing well. He just ate some food and now we will ... Oh God, Linda, I am so sorry!" Veronica says before Linda begins to sob pitifully.

The two ladies remain silent on the phone before hearing a voice scream "TIME IS UP!"

"I guess that demand goes out to me," Linda says trying to make a joke of the situation. Before I go, please take care of Zach until this whole ordeal is over. I know that he is in good hands with you, but I need you to know if things get bad you can go to the apartment and help yourself to whatever you may need. I've always pictured you as family."

"Don't worry about that right now. More important is that you take care of yourself and that baby. Inform me as soon as you hear of getting released. Zacori is in good hands. I will treat him as if he is mine."

"I know! I will call you soon. Take care. Bye," says Linda before hanging up the phone.

Veronica hangs up and sits for a minute just looking at Zacori innocently playing on the floor. She runs her fingers through his hair, all the while thinking *How can someone hurt something so precious?* The more she sits, the more she indulges in the idea of being a mom. For now, taking care of Zacori is a great way for her to begin practicing. Unable to help herself from joining in, she kneels to the floor and grabs a car.

"It's just you and me for now," she says.

The next morning after taking Zacori to preschool, Veronica heads to the courtroom to support the Burnses while they wait to be arraigned. Once she arrives inside after going through a series of metal detectors, she enters the courtroom where she sees Linda and Mr. Burns on a bench huddled together whispering to their lawyer. *I wonder what that conversation is about – I'm sure it's not a good one*, she thinks as she catches Linda's attention when she turns her head. They quickly wave hello to each other before the bailiff calls Linda's name.

"ALL RISE!" screams the bailiff as the judge enters the courtroom before sitting in her chair.

"Please be seated," the judge announces to the court. "In the case of the state of New York vs. John and Linda Burns on the charges of kidnapping, human trafficking and soliciting prostitution, how do the defendants plead?"

"Not guilty, Your Honor. Also, the defense would like to advise the court that in fact there were originally charges of child abuse against their nanny after a video proved abuse of their now three-year-old son. The state is only making an attempt to ignore the welfare of a child, hoping it will bring them some leniency against the nanny in the case against their son. This is a mere distraction, Your Honor," their attorney says.

"Your Honor, the state asks that no bail be set due to the financial status of the defendants who could possibly become flight risks. The defendants have many high-profile business associates in other countries that will gladly harbor them to escape our justice system. Also, the state would like to advise the court that we believe the nanny only rebelled after years of abuse and sexual relations with Mr. Burns," says the prosecutor.

"Your Honor, we ask that the court take into consideration the health status of Mrs. Burns at this time and acknowledge that my client has no interest in leaving at this stage of pregnancy," the defense attorney pleads.

"The court will consider the health of Mrs. Burns and post her bail at $1 million. As far as Mr. Burns, he will remain in custody of the Department of Corrections until trial begins a month from this date. It is so ordered," the judge says. She slams the gavel and proceeds to walk out of the courtroom.

Mr. Burns stands and whispers into his lawyer's ear before turning to Linda and giving her a hug to assure her it will be fine. Linda hugs her husband before the corrections officers escort him out of the courtroom. She looks behind her to see Veronica with a look of sorrow and asks a female officer if it is OK to say something quickly before going back into trial booking.

The officer agrees to give her a minute. Veronica approaches the swinging door and hugs the waiting arms of Linda.

"I am so sorry!" Veronica says.

"Thank you, but we can't worry about the past right now. I need you to do something for me. At the apartment by the second entrance there is a key you can use to enter. Once inside, go to the guest bedroom and behind the family portrait there you will find the code to the safe on the floor of the closet in the master bedroom. You will find what you need to get me out of here. Thank you so much," says Linda.

While exiting the courtroom, Veronica notices a group of possibly Chinese men huddled in the corner whispering among themselves. *They must be the business partners of Mr. Burns here to support him,* she thinks to herself. It is still hard for her to believe exactly what is going on, but more importantly, it is time to make her way downtown to help Linda. The quicker she leaves, the faster she will be able to bail her out so Zacori can see his mom.

Two hours later Veronica arrives at the apartment, and everything is exactly where Linda said it would be. She finally understands what Linda said the afternoon she was arrested; that she felt Veronica was family and could be trusted with her most precious things. She searches through the house following every instruction Linda relayed to her until she comes upon the safe. Once it's opened, Veronica's eyes roll as she looks at the cash the Burns have in their home.

Who keeps this amount of money in their house? She asks herself while gathering enough to bail Linda out. Looking at more money than she has or will probably ever see in her life, she thinks about what would happen if she were to take a little extra for herself. *Who would really know? I can help my family and myself out so much,* she thinks. She picks up a slab of 100s and looks at it closely before throwing it in the bag. *It's not right. I will only take what I need to help Linda.* After taking the necessary 10% to post Linda's bail, Veronica begins to make her way out of the apartment. She puts the keys back behind the picture before she is interrupted by what seems to be voices entering the apartment. Tiptoeing to the door, she slowly peeks through the crack, noticing three men speaking a foreign language rumbling through the apartment.

Oh my God. What am I going to do? I know they're not here to bail anybody out, she thinks to herself, beginning to panic while trying to find someplace to hide. The only thing she can think of is going back into the closet. Quietly waiting for the men to continue searching through the apartment for whatever they came for, Veronica can only think of the worst if she were to be found. As one of the men approaches the bedroom to search, she begins to pray with her eyes closed, opening an eye every few seconds to see how close the man is. The closer he comes, the faster she prays.

He reaches the closet and it seems as if time stands still for a moment as he attempts to open the door. He tugs twice and Veronica grabs an umbrella to prepare for a fight. The light from the bedroom begins to break through the door the more he opens it. Her heart is pounding so rapidly she can hear it as it presses firmly against her ribcage. Each breath becomes shallower as the unknown comes closer.

"Oh my goodness!" she whispers repeatedly. Suddenly he stops. The other men have called him back into the other room. Obviously they've found what they were desperately searching for as they overlook documents before exiting. "Thank you, God!" she says before leaving the closet.

She hesitates for a few minutes before walking through the apartment contemplating if she should call the police or just leave. It would be extremely suspicious that she's there just hours after her boss was sent to jail with a bag full of 100s. Without hesitation, she grabs the bag of money and leaves immediately, heading to the bank for a cashier's check.

An hour later Veronica enters the bank. Since it is for a large amount, she has to sit and wait to speak to someone behind the desk. A young woman walks over and introduces herself as Susan before sitting down to review the paperwork. "Wow, this is a large amount of money. I'm sorry – I didn't catch your name," Susan asks.

Veronica pauses for a moment, knowing Susan must be very suspicious of how she came to the bank to purchase a large cashier's check without having an account there. In order for this to happen she really has to think quickly. Because of Mr. Burns' reputation in the city, she hopes mentioning his name will have some advantage if Susan has ever met him.

"I am really surprised that Linda has never mentioned me. I am Veronica, the nanny of the Burnses who live down here in Chelsea, the owners of the Fabric House," she says, hoping the lady will automatically be in agreement.

"No, I can't really recall ever hearing of you, but I definitely know John and Linda. I do know that an Asian woman came in here a few times with Linda and their son." Susan hesitates.

"Zacori? Blond hair and the biggest blue eyes imaginable?" Veronica responds, bringing a smile to the lady's face.

"Yes! That's his name. Zacori. Are the things that I have been hearing about Mr. Burns true? What actually happened?" she asks.

"Well, it's all accusations for now, but they're being held at this time. And with poor Linda being pregnant, it is really no place for her to be, so that is what brings me here. All I know is..." Veronica begins to tell the story to the representative while leaning closer so she can be heard. After fifteen minutes of telling Susan the story, she lifts her head up with tears in her eyes.

"That's just disrespectful! Do you need all of this, or does she need more?" Susan asks.

"I believe that would cover all she needs to get out. I will be bailing her out as soon as possible," says Veronica.

"No problem. Please, let Linda know if she needs anything or just a helping hand, don't hesitate to reach out to me," says Susan. After Susan finishes all the paperwork, she hands Veronica an envelope with her card attached and gives her hug. She remains standing, shaking her head watching Veronica walk out of the bank.

Chapter 9

The next morning, Veronica receives a call from Keith telling her that he will be returning from his meeting with her parents. He expresses to her that a lot of things will be different once he returns, as far their relationship is concerned.

"How are you?" he asks.

"I guess I'm fine. There's just so much going on right now that I need to tell you about," she says.

"What's wrong?" Keith asks, concerned.

Veronica tells Keith of the incident with the Burns and that she is now taking care of Zacori until she is able to bail Linda out of jail later on today. She also informs him of the near-death situation she put herself in while getting the bail money for Linda from her Chelsea loft.

"Wow! That's a lot for one person to handle in a short matter of time. I really need you to be extremely careful until I get home. Sometimes in business you have to make decisions that can be extremely dangerous to stay in control," says Keith. "I'll be home tomorrow, and I hope you are available to see me!"

"Of course I'll be able to," Veronica responds.

"I love you!"

"I love you too," she says before hanging up the phone. Turning to look into the doorway, she notices Zacori standing there rubbing his eyes, trying to fully awaken.

"How long have you been standing there?" she asks while walking over to pick him up. "We have to get you ready for pre-school, little man, before I go to work."

After getting off the train a few blocks away from the job, she notices fire trucks and the smell of smoke lingering in the air. Not paying too much attention to it, Veronica looks at her watch to make sure she will be on time. *Mr. Burns may not be in, but knowing him, he would ask to check the time sheets from a corrections officer's phone*, she jokingly thinks to herself. Approaching the building, she is stopped by a barricade set up by the police redirecting pedestrians across the street and notices all of her co-workers bunched together, looking up in amazement. She turns to the place once called her job, now engulfed in flames with firefighters desperately trying to control the blaze.

While some stand in shock trying to figure out how this happened, Veronica wonders if there is a connection between the fire and what she experienced yesterday. *I wonder what exactly Mr. Burns has done for some of his achievements, but whatever he did, he is definitely paying for it now*, she thinks to herself, watching her job go up in flames.

As sad as it is to see what is happening, there is a bigger agenda that needs to be handled today. There is still the fact that Linda has to be released from jail and kept safe amidst all that's happening.

"Agnes, you have my number. Can you please keep me informed on how things turn out?" Veronica asks.

"There is no need to see how things turn out; you're looking at it. Thirty years of my life going up in flames. It was all I knew. It provided me with overtime to put my kids through college when my husband died. I slept in that very basement when I didn't have rent money," Agnes says, shaking her head watching the building burn.

Veronica is speechless trying to imagine the pain Agnes must be feeling. Not until today did she realize how some people see a job as just a way to make money, while others see it as all they have. "I can't say I understand how you feel, but things will work out. Maybe you can start over," she says in an attempt to ease the pain.

"Start over? Start over! I'm a 67-year-old white woman who stayed loyal to where I started. In my generation, you stayed loyal to the job that gave you a chance. When we found a job, we found a new family. I have watched people I started here with die and seen generations of kids come and go in that very same building burning over there. This was my 'look forward to tomorrow' place, but I wouldn't expect you or anyone else here to understand that. Just go! You and all these border runners. I don't need this. Excuse me!" Agnes angrily says before walking through the crowd to make her way down the street.

Knowing this may be the last time she will ever see Agnes and that there is nothing she can do gives Veronica a sense of helplessness. But today it is all about Linda. She glances at her watch and proceeds to walk toward the subway.

Now at the courthouse, Veronica begins to complete all the paperwork that is necessary to process Linda's bail. The young lady behind the bulletproof glass periodically looks up at Veronica while rolling her eyes and speaking to her in an aggressive tone.

"Is there something wrong?" Veronica asks.

"Why? Does it look like something is wrong?" the lady quickly responds.

Veronica hesitates for a moment, knowing her words can affect the release of Linda. "No, I just wanted to ask if you were OK. Your body language and tone give me the impression you may be feeling a certain way about me," Veronica explains.

"I'm fine. It just never seems to amaze me that all you sisters hurry down here and bail all your white friends out immediately, but can only visit your brothers who are here for no reason. Just a bunch of sellouts if you ask me. Here are your papers," she says, tossing them through the little space provided at the bottom of the glass, causing the papers to fall in disarray to the floor.

Veronica is speechless after hearing the hurtful words that came from the receptionist's mouth. She stands there with her fist tightly wrapped in her pocket. No matter how she wants to sock the woman for her ignorance, she knows it isn't about her. "And you wonder why nobody asked you," she says sarcastically as she picks the papers up from the floor.

After nearly waiting for an hour, Linda finally appears from the back unshackled. She looks up and smiles at Veronica as she exits the gloomy cells of the jail. As the two greet, they embrace with an overwhelming hug.

"Thank you so much," says Linda. "I don't know what I would've done if you weren't around."

"That's OK. But I think we should first go to my apartment, have you take a hot shower and talk before picking up Zacori. There are a lot of things that have happened since you have been in here that you really need to know about."

"A shower sounds like a great idea. Let's just get out of here. I have seen enough of this filth to last me a lifetime," Linda says, putting on her jacket.

As the two ladies begin to exit the courthouse, Veronica pauses. "Linda, can you just meet me by the door? I think I forgot something on the receptionist's desk." She approaches the desk where the receptionist arrogantly sits with her arms folded.

"Excuse me, sister. I just wanted to inform you that whatever you may think in your enslaved mentality of black people who have true friends of other races, you're wrong. She's my friend, and the color of real friends doesn't matter," says Veronica.

"Whoop Dee doo! A sister with a white friend. Should I want to be close to you now?" the receptionist says.

"No! You should just focus on my finger as I leave." Veronica walks with her head up high and her middle finger placed firmly in the small of her back. She places her arm around Linda and together they leave the courthouse.

After a few hours, the two ladies unwind and Veronica tells Linda of the things she has learned from her experience at the apartment and the burning of the main building. Linda, shocked by some of the things she hears, can only blankly stare to the ceiling in disbelief. "What in the world was this man truly into? How could I have been so blind?" she says.

"It will be fine. The most important thing is that now you're out and you can take care of yourself and Zacori, and that's a great thing," Veronica says.

"I always knew that his success would come with a price, but I thought it was just sacrificing time with family. Never did I expect this. This is crazy. What am I going to do now?" Linda says before laying her head on Veronica's shoulder.

"I know this may be extremely difficult right now, and I can't put myself in your shoes, but the most important thing to focus on now is yours and Zacori's safety. You are very welcome – no, I insist that you stay here until things cool down a little. Keith is coming home soon and I can stay with him," Veronica says.

Linda begins to laugh. "Who would have thought I would meet someone so loving over a cup of coffee? Thank you."

"It's my pleasure. Don't worry, I will be here with you every step of the way," Veronica expresses to Linda.

⁓

It's been a few weeks since everything has happened, and the trial against Mr. Burns is getting ready to begin. At this point Linda is almost in the clear according to the meetings she has held with her lawyer. Most, if not all the charges are aimed at Mr. Burns, who in order to clear Linda's name has confessed that she has had nothing to do with his business transactions or relationship with Ming. She spends a lot of time wondering what she's going to do now, looking at her stomach crying. Veronica, understanding how stressful this is on her friend, has begun to spend more time with Linda just listening to her talk or holding hands in silence.

A horn blows continually from outside the window of Veronica's apartment. It's Keith, who is going for support, signaling to the ladies that he has arrived. Today starts with Ming's testimony. Linda seems to be in good spirits, but Veronica can tell it is tearing her apart. Now eight months pregnant, she waddles her way from the back. "Alright, already! Tell Keith I just can't move as I used to," she says while trying to keep a smile on her face. Veronica helps her put on her coat and they exit the apartment.

Later that afternoon, the three of them wait in the courtroom for the trial to begin. This time, the courtroom is giving Veronica the chills. "Is it me, or is it extremely emotionless and cold in here?" she asks.

"It has to be. Any minute, Satan is going to walk through the door and heat things up," Linda comments.

The court officers open the rear door to the courtroom, escorting Mr. Burns, shackled at his hands and feet in a custom-made Armani suit, to his seat next to his attorney. "Speak of the devil, and he shall appear. Well at least they have him in cuffs," says Linda. "He looks so distant, different almost."

"Even in jail, the man wears a thousand-dollar suit," Keith whispers to Veronica.

Linda briefly waves hello, only to be greeted with a smirk of worry from Mr. Burns. He sits in his chair as the corrections officer releases the shackles from his hands. He shakes his lawyer's hand and begins to write on his yellow note pad.

"ALL RISE!" a voice yells, signaling the arrival of the judge. Veronica clutches Linda's hand and looks at her to make her feel more at ease, doing the same to Keith.

"Are you ready for this?" Veronica asks.

"Ready or not, it's too late now," says Linda before the courtroom is instructed to be seated.

"Ladies and gentlemen of the jury, before we begin and call our first witness to the stand, I would like for you to remember that we are here today to put an end to the inhumane trafficking of innocent women for the profit of a criminal enterprise supported by the rich and evil. We will prove that the actions preceding the abuse of the defendant's child were only in revenge for the physical and emotional abuse that was caused to our first witness. By no means do the true victim or we deny the crimes she has committed, but we are here to help you understand the circumstances that led up to it. In saying that, we call our first VICTIM to the stand, Xiao Xing Ming," says the attorney before Ming enters the courtroom escorted by a female court officer.

Linda clutches Veronica's hands when she sees Ming, who remains staring at the ground before entering into the witness stand and taking her oath.

"I wish I could just kill her," Linda mumbles under her breath. Veronica shakes her hand to assure her it will be OK.

"Before we begin, I would just like the jury to understand who you are and where you're from. Also, if you don't mind, give us a little background on how you arrived to the U.S. and what the conditions were once you got here," says the attorney.

"My real name is Xiao Xing Ming and I was originally born in North Korea. I was 10 when my sister and I where taken away to China by a group of men as we were walking home from school.

"And what happened after that?"

"We were originally transported from one place to another, usually forced to doing manual labor in warehouses until we got a little older."

"And then? Once you became older?" the attorney asks.

"I can remember being placed in a large, cold room with mattresses to sleep on with other young women and periodically seeing young girls taken out, only some returning. It didn't take long for me to realize I would never see my parents again. I just didn't want to lose my sister. She was a little older than me and developed, and there were times they would take her away for a few hours. She would return half dressed and tired. I wanted to help her as much as I could, but I was too young to do anything."

"And what ever happened to her, your sister?" the prosecutor asks.

"I don't know. One day they came for her and she never came back," Ming says, looking down to the floor as tears begin to fall from her eyes. She lifts her head, pulling her hair back before taking a tissue from the box in front of her.

"From the years that you were held against your will, at what age would you say a young woman is sold or forced into prostitution?"

"It is not until the age of 16 that we're forced to do sexual favors or sell our bodies until we have made enough money for the person who owns us, to let us free."

"Were there many women of different races and cultures where you were held captive?" the prosecutor asks.

"I've met a lot of women over the years, women from India, Africa, all the way to Brazil. From time to time, I would see a white woman come in, but they never stayed long."

"Why?"

"The Middle Eastern men would usually pre-order them, so when the type of American white woman they requested was taken, she would sell immediately. It was important to hurry and get these women as far from where they are taken in order for the U.S. government not to get involved. The rest of us usually suffered until we either overdosed or were let go when they were finished with us."

"Did that make you feel any kind of way about Mrs. Burns?"

"No. I felt sorry for her, actually. I knew she knew nothing of what was really going on."

"Have you ever been in a relationship of any kind with the defendant?"

"Yes."

"Pregnant?"

"Yes."

Linda sits there in amazement as whispers now fill the once quiet courtroom. She glances over to Mr. Burns, who sits emotionless about the accusations brought up against him.

"When did your affairs with Mr. Burns begin? And at what age did you first become pregnant?"

"I first met John ten years ago while he was on business in China. He was very kind and gentle in the beginning, and our

80

relationship was not sexual at all. I didn't know if he was married, but it really didn't matter if he was anyway. We just talked a lot, and he visited me often when he came to China on business."

"Is that when the affair began?"

"Yes! It was never for money. I wanted to. He was charming and gentle. He promised me a different life than what I was used to. With him I was not a prostitute or a call girl. During our time together, he made me feel special. There were many women for him to choose from, but he always requested me."

"Did you love him?"

"Yes."

"From the time you met the defendant until now, how many times have you been pregnant?"

Ming hesitates for a minute to look up at Mrs. Burns, who is staring curiously at her. "Three. But never was I able to carry it to term. I was always forced to have abortions."

"By whom? And if you don't mind, please point to whomever that person maybe if they are in this courtroom." the lawyer asks.

"I was pregnant four months ago. And it was Mr. Burns' child," Ming responds as she points in Mr. Burns' direction.

"Oh my God!" Linda says while hearing Ming's testimony. She covers her mouth to silence the painful moans of sorrow that are overwhelming her emotionally. Mascara-tinged tears drip to her white shirt. Her lips quiver uncontrollably as her legs shake. She looks at Veronica, who can do no more than shake her head, as she's also crying. "This can't be true," she says while looking over at her husband, who remains in his chair writing on a pad, periodically whispering to his lawyer.

Meanwhile Ming continues to answer without hesitation every question asked by the D.A.

"When you came to the states, was it made possible by Mr. Burns?"

"Yes."

"What did he promise you?"

"He told me we would have a life together and a family. He told me that he was married and very unhappy, but I needed to be patient until he got a divorce."

"At what point did he ask you to come into his home and care for his son?"

"He told me to do that so he could keep an eye on me. He wanted me to be close. I never was happy about the idea, so I remained silent most of the time around his wife. I never meant to hurt his wife or son."

"What brought you to placing your hands on their child?"

Ming remains silent. The courtroom has become extremely quiet, once again awaiting her response. If there is anything of the utmost importance, this is it.

"After he began to abuse me."

"Abusing you? Are you telling the court that Mr. Burns began to physically abuse you?"

"Yes."

"Can you tell us when this physical abuse began?"

"I told him if he didn't leave his wife I'd tell her about us. He became so angry he slapped me repeatedly in my face and reminded me that I could easily be put on a 'whore boat' back to China. Every time I looked at Zacori, I thought about the children I was forced to abort so his life could remain the same. I knew what I was before, but he promised me different, and I believed him. Finally realizing the truth about him and knowing I was free from prostitution but not slavery angered me. I never meant to hurt the child, but my anger toward Mr. Burns spilled over to my actions toward Zacori. I am so sorry for that," says Ming before wiping the tears that have begun to run down her face.

"I can't do this right now. I am starting to feel really sick. I need some air," says Linda as she stands up and turns into the aisle to exit. Veronica immediately follows her after excusing herself from Keith.

Mr. Burns realizes Linda's leaving and stands. "LINDA!" he yells, only to see her continue out the door.

"Sit down. NOW!" the court officer says, placing his hand on Mr. Burns' arm firmly.

Once outside, Linda sits on a bench fanning herself, taking in slow, deep breaths to calm herself down.

"Are you OK?" Veronica asks.

"I guess. Just a little overwhelmed right now with all that I just heard. I can't believe he would have the balls to bring a woman he actually had relations with into our home and around our family."

Veronica places her arm around Linda's shoulders and grabs her close.

"What's so amazing to me right now is that I don't even know why I am crying. Every thought that I ever had about the business trips, late night dinners and meetings has just come to light. I mean, look at my Christmas parties. They were basically hooker reunions, now that I think about it. How could I have been so stupid?"

"I will not tell you that it's OK, but I will say that it's not your fault. You had absolutely no idea of what was happening," says Veronica.

"Sure it is! I blinded myself from the reality of my family and surroundings with the fear of not living well off. What held no value was more valuable to me than the welfare of my child and relationship with my husband. I am as guilty as Ming," Linda says looking straight ahead.

"Don't say that. You should..."

Linda quickly interrupts. "I think the best thing for me to do right now is just go back to your place and lie down. I really just need to rest."

"OK, I understand. Let me just tell Keith to get the car and we can make our way."

"That won't be necessary. I will take a small stroll and then catch a cab. Plus, I need you here to keep me informed on how this circus turns out," Linda replies.

"Fine. I will see you back at the apartment once this is over. Be careful, sister!"

Linda pauses for a moment as she looks to Veronica, obviously caught off guard by the remark she just made. "I could not have said it better, sister," she says before waddling toward the front door of the courthouse. As she opens the door and turns to wave goodbye, the rays of sun reflect on her as if a halo is hovering over her head. She proceeds to exit with Veronica heading back into the courtroom, where Keith awaits her return.

Veronica sits and takes a deep breath. "Did I miss anything?" she asks.

"You were already here when she confessed to the affair. Now they have presented documents for the apartment he leased for her in his name and confiscated bank receipts to prove he paid the rent, so now his attorney is speaking with the judge. My guess is that he understands he is done and wants to make a plea with the courts," Keith explains.

Mr. Burns sits in his chair, nervously searching the courtroom for someone or something.

"How's Linda?" Keith asks.

"A little distraught after hearing the testimony of course, so she decided to just go back to the apartment and rest. I can only imagine how she may be feeling right now after hearing that her spouse had a whole other lifestyle," says Veronica.

"There are always two sides and before we rush to..." The judge calling for silence in the courtroom, signaling he will begin to speak interrupts Keith. Both lawyers return to their seats and stand by their clients.

"In light of the recent testimony that we have heard from Ms. Ming, counsel has opted to no longer proceed with a trial hearing. There will be a plea deal which both parties have deemed fair. Am I correct?" the judge asks.

"Yes, Your Honor," the prosecutor says.

"And for the defendant?"

Mr. Burns' lawyer is still trying to reason with Mr. Burns, who suddenly shakes his head in agreement.

"Yes, Your Honor," the defense lawyer says. "My client has agreed to plead guilty to the charges brought before him and fully accepts the plea bargain deal offered."

The courtroom is in total shock at the sudden change of events that has just taken place. Veronica can only sit there with her hand covering her mouth, speechless at what she just heard. "What does that mean, Keith?" she asks.

"It means he just realized things aren't going to turn out good for him, so he's confessing in hopes that the court will show him mercy. In other words, he's screwed," Keith, says.

"Order in the court!" screams the judge.

In light of the recent change of events, the judge dismisses the jury and thanks them for their service. "After the jury has left the courtroom, we will proceed with the terms of the agreement," states the judge.

The jury stands to be escorted from the courtroom by the court officers.

"The state has agreed to drop the charges of kidnapping and soliciting prostitution for the maximum sentence of harboring illegal immigrants in the United States," says the prosecutor.

"Do both parties agree to the deal set?"

"Yes we do," both attorneys, say simultaneously.

Mr. Burns' attorney gestures for him to stand, but he begins to feel weak as he rises. It's obvious at this point that the seriousness of his situation has now become a reality. The attorney lends him a helping hand to his feet.

"Mr. Burns, on the charges of harboring illegal immigrants in violation of the Labor Law Act of the United States, you are hereby sentenced to 15 years in federal prison, which will begin immediately once you are turned over to custody of the U.S. marshal. Also, Ms. Ming will return to the custody of the Department of Corrections until her trial begins. It is so ordered," the judge says, hammering his gavel.

Mr. Burns whispers a few words to his attorney before placing his hands behind his back to be handcuffed. He turns, looking in the direction where Linda and Veronica were sitting, realizing his wife is gone, then nods his head to his business partners standing in the rear of the courtroom. He is biting his bottom lip and shaking his head toward the ground as the marshals take him away.

A few people remain in the courtroom, obviously whispering amongst themselves about the chain of events that just occurred, especially the distinguished businessmen who were once partners of Mr. Burns, possibly the sole reason he's just lost everything he ever worked for.

"I wonder what's going on in their minds right now," Keith asks.

"Whatever it is, that verdict looks as if it will definitely shake things up a little bit," Veronica responds as they glance toward them. Come on, honey. I still have to find a way to explain this to Linda before Zacori comes from school."

"I think I'll go with you. She can use all the support she can get right now. Let's go," Keith says before leaving the courtroom.

Veronica and Keith arrive at the apartment building. It's taken them longer than usual, as they've tried to find a way to tell Linda the tragic outcome that occurred in court.

"How do you think she is going to take it?"

"I don't know, and that is what scares me the most. For God's sake, she is eight months pregnant. Whether she's ready to hear it or I'm ready to tell her, we're here now, and it must be said," Veronica says approaching the apartment door.

She opens the door slowly as she and Keith enter the apartment. As they walk through the corridor, Keith gestures that he will go to the back and give the two ladies a little alone time to talk. Veronica continues toward the living room, where she notices Linda sitting silently on the couch. She softly calls her name as she approaches, but there is no response. *Maybe she is taking a short nap. She did say that she was exhausted with everything in the courthouse.* Veronica takes a deep breath and puts on a quick smile before playfully turning to the couch.

"Linda! You don't hear me calling you?" Veronica stops as she realizes Linda is sitting on the couch pale-faced with her eyes rolled to the back of her head and dried blood accumulated around her wrist. "No, no! Linda!" she screams. She places her finger to Linda's throat to check for her pulse. "Keith!" she screams out hysterically.

Running from the back, Keith reaches the couch and covers his mouth in disbelief at the scene he is witnessing. "Oh my God!" is all he can say as he reaches for his cell phone to call 911.

Veronica cradles her cold friend looking for an answer. "How could you? How could you?" she asks.

"The police are on their way," Keith says. "Come on babe! She's gone," he says, slowly releasing Veronica's grip on Linda.

"Why, Keith? Why would she do this? It was going to be OK, Linda!" she cries.

"I don't know. I wish I had an answer for you." At that moment, he looks toward the table where two envelopes were placed, one addressed to Veronica and the other Zacori. He picks one envelope up and opens the letter, quickly glancing over the words inside. It is from Linda.

"I guess this tells you some of the reasons why," he says before passing it over to a distraught Veronica, who slowly gets herself together and sits it the chair adjacent to the couch. Keith places his arm around her shoulder as Veronica begins to read the letter aloud:

My Dearest Sister:

By the time you read this, the thoughts running through your mind are probably unimaginable looking at me on this couch. I can only be honest with you and hope that you will one day understand why I would do this to myself. I gave up. I couldn't find the strength to deal with the embarrassment and lack of self-worth I was feeling. To realize that I put the materialistic objects of life on a higher pedestal than being a good mother as my everyday interest, I was selfish. Afraid of being poor again and looked at as a failure and freeloader with my kids having to deal with an uneducated mother who didn't have what it would take to provide a comfortable life, I couldn't become a woman with no future, raising children in the same system that failed her. I pray that you never have to go through the pain and hurt I went through with my husband. Always remember, you can forget a lie, but never forgive being deceived. Even though my lungs breathed air and my heart pumped blood, it traveled in a hollow shell. The weaker the heart gets, the emptier the soul becomes. I know God will never bless me or forgive this sin I have committed, but I pray that you will forgive me for my actions. As selfish as it may sound, I couldn't bring another child into this world of bitterness and lies. They say children are the closest we can ever get to God, so I ask that you always take care of my angel Zacori and that God be with you. You are the only person who I know will love him as your own and care for him, as a strong mother should. It didn't take me years to realize it was you that I have been waiting for to leave. There is going to come a day when he will ask questions that you may not be able to answer. I am leaving this letter for you to give to him once you think he will truly understand why I am not around. I love you, sister! And I'm sorry.

Love always, Linda

Veronica looks up at Keith, who remains speechless shaking his head. They sit on the floor nestled together staring at Linda's body.

Chapter 10

Life with Zacori

It's been three years since the tragic suicide of Linda and sentencing of Mr. Burns. In the beginning Veronica would periodically receive letters from Mr. Burns, but even that has ended now. After the imprisonment of Mr. Burns, it didn't take long before the Fabric House enterprise went belly up. The mismanagement of funds and absence of proper leadership led the company to close all its doors and file bankruptcy after only two years.

Playing the role of a full-time mom has become extremely difficult for Veronica, but there is no way she is going to allow Zacori to be in the system that has failed so many other children. Keith has been very supportive financially since Zacori has been in the custody of Veronica, but his traveling more frequently to Africa now leaves her thinking about their personal relationship. Is he with her because of love, or does he feels obligated to stay because of the circumstances?

Sitting in the living room of her apartment, Veronica stares out the window wondering where her life is headed. She can't help but to feel as if things have gone backward. The economy has made a sudden change for the worst. She is once again unemployed and now has the responsibility of raising a six-year-old kid whose parents left her with no financial assistance. It is a struggle, but no matter how hard things are, there is one purpose that makes her continue moving forward, and that is Zacori. She would have never imagined the amount of love and drive to be successful a person could develop until having a child.

Her life has changed in ways that she never thought imaginable. To love someone as much as she loves herself is amazing to her. It is also very challenging, especially walking down the street with Zacori and hearing the remarks from people as they observe them together. The blacks call her a sell out and others merely look and smirk, but she knows what that means. Even in the school Zacori attends, the teachers sometimes assume she's the nanny. She plays the role to keep the school from asking too many questions.

Every night like clockwork, Veronica has Zacori say a little prayer for his parents' return. She knows that Zacori is too young to understand or truly comprehend what happened, so she simply told him they went away on a trip and would return soon. Since there are no other family members to tell him different, her story has never been disputed.

Tonight is going to be a very special night. Keith is scheduled to return from his business trip and has expressed to her that there is something very important and life changing he must share with her. This is great news for Veronica. If there is anyone who has been supportive of all she is doing and going through, it is Keith. He is her rock. All night she anticipates what it is he needs to talk about. *There is only one thing so important that he can't wait to talk about,* she thinks to herself, hoping this is the day he will finally ask her to marry him. With that thought, she practices saying yes repeatedly in the mirror. If having Zacori over the last three years has proved anything, it's definitely showed her what she is missing by not having children of her own.

It's 8 p.m. and Keith has finally called to say he will be arriving between 9 and 9:30 p.m. Veronica rushes to get Zacori to bed so she can have a little time to freshen up before Keith arrives. Putting on a beautiful nightgown along with the perfume he loves, Veronica sits on the couch with Sade playing softly in the back and Riesling chilling on ice. She hears keys fiddling at the door before the hallway light begins to fill the front corridor. She moves nervously to fluff up pillows, getting herself in the sexiest position she can think of. This man saved her from a brutal rape, took a trip to Ghana to meet her parents, and supported her mentally and financially in her decision to take care of her ex-boss' abandoned child. She loves Keith with all her soul and is ready to prove it.

Quickly gulping down a glass of wine before he enters the room, she looks up and there he is. The light from the hallway only allows her to see his frame. She stands to her feet with open arms to greet him with a hug as he places his bags to the floor. She runs to his awaiting arms like a child to their parent and wraps her legs around his waist, burying her head in his neck. For five minutes they simply embrace each other without saying a word. Finally letting go, Veronica looks Keith over thoroughly, noticing he doesn't have on the traditional power suit he usually wears while on business. This time he's returned wearing a dishdasha, which is usually worn by Muslim men, with sandals on his feet.

"Wow, you look great, but I think I just realized what your big surprise could be," she says.

"Do you really think so? Do you?" Keith asks with so much cheer in his voice. "Please sit. There is so much I really need to explain to you about this trip."

Veronica bashfully covers her exposed cleavage while clearing her throat and pouring another glass of wine.

"The first thing is that this trip to Ghana was the most important for me. Not only was I able to do great business, but I was finally granted a meeting with the elders of my old village to enter Islam," Keith says. "I know this maybe a total shock to you, but I kept it secret until I was really sure it was going to happen."

"So what does this mean?" she asks.

"It means that I have converted to Islam, and that was only one of the reasons why I traveled back home so frequently. The second reason was to pick this up for you." Keith reaches down into his pocket and pulls out a small box.

Veronica attempts to be as calm as possible when she sees the box. This is the moment that she has been waiting for since the day they reunited in the park. He slides off the couch and goes down on one knee, grabbing her hand. Veronica yells "Yes!" before Keith can get a word out.

They laugh as tears slowly roll down her face. Keith wipes her eyes before repositioning himself on the floor to propose finally. "I have waited a long time for this day, hoping I would be able to find a woman with all the qualities that I have searched for during my years on this earth. Now I will never say I am perfect, but you have changed me into a better person and I can't take the risk of losing that. So, I ask you – no, I beg you to finish completing me. Will you marry me?"

"Yes!" Veronica responds as Keith slides the ring on her finger. He stands back to his feet, grabbing her hand and gently kissing her on the lips. They quietly embrace each other, enjoying the moment before Veronica feels a tug on her leg. There stands Zacori, holding his blanket before Keith picks him up into his arms. "There is one more important thing to remember. I want you to understand that I am a package deal now and..."

Keith places his finger to her lips to silence her. "I will treat Zacori as if I helped birth him myself. I just hope one day when our children come, he will understand his brothers and sisters with an open mind," he says.

"Thank you. I appreciate that," she says before leaning over to kiss him. Together they stand as a family. As Veronica goes to the back to put Zacori to bed, Keith thinks about how he will try to explain to Veronica the importance of her converting to Islam. His phone rings. He looks down at the phone and realizes it is a call from Africa. He peaks his head over the couch to see if Veronica is returning before he answers the call.

"Hello," he answers as a woman begins to speak. "I know, I know! Yes, I made it back safely. I was meaning to call, but as soon as my flight landed it was back to business as usual. Where are the children? Are they in bed yet? OK, I love you too."

The room door from the back closing signals to Keith that Veronica is returning. He hurries to rush off the phone. "I will call you as soon as I get settled. Tomorrow when I come from work, I will send the money that I promised." Veronica enters the room. Keith begins to speak as if he's holding a conversation with his mother as Veronica sits on the couch next to him.

"No, no, don't worry, mother. I will call you as soon as I finish getting rest tomorrow. Love you too. Bye!"

"Who was that?"

"It was my mother. You know how some are, even when their youngest children are adults, they still treat them as toddlers," Keith says laughing as Veronica softly pushes him.

"Hey! Watch it buddy."

"What I wanted to talk to you about is my converting to Islam and how important it is for you, I mean us, of course." He re-positions himself on the couch. "In order for us to truly receive the blessings of Allah, I have to ask if you would ever think of converting from being a Christian."

"Wow! That's really something to discuss. My family was raised to be Christians, and we are still faithful to those beliefs today. I'm sorry, but I don't know if I can do that," she explains.

"I understand. I truly do, and I am not trying to say that my new way of religious practice is the only way or the best way for all. But, I can only ask for our future and our children's, that you open your mind to Islam and invite new ideas and beliefs for us to truly unite in this marriage," Keith says trying to convince Veronica.

Hesitant to answer, Veronica looks down at her ring, twisting it with her fingers.

Keith grabs her hand. "For us?"

"I guess I can give it a try and be supportive. I will have to be honest. I don't want you to believe I will automatically convert over from being a Christian, but if it is something you strongly believe in, I am willing to put my personal feelings aside to stand by you with an open mind," she says.

"That is the reason I love you!" Keith says, rising to his feet and lifting Veronica into his arms. He heads toward the bedroom with Veronica in his arms like a newly married couple would cross the threshold. He places her on the bed and turns to close the door. Before closing the door, he notices Zacori standing in the hallway with his blanket around his arms, looking in the direction of their bedroom. Their eyes lock momentarily. Zacori smiles as he begins to walk towards the room before the slamming of the door suddenly halts him. Hopelessly he stands in the dark hallway with only the moonlight allowing him to see. He lies on the floor quietly and wraps the blanket over his body, feeling desolate listening to the moans and giggles echoing from the bedroom.

Chapter 11

I t's taken Keith a month to get Veronica to agree to visit a mosque for the first time. Since they are in Manhattan, the 96th Street mosque that was recommended by some of Keith's friends is his first choice. Initially, Veronica is very uncomfortable walking into the mosque knowing how strongly her family would feel about it and her own thoughts about other religions. But, she did promise Keith that she would give it a chance, and she believes in him.

Upon entering the mosque, they are greeted by a middle-aged man of Arabic descent with a long beard dressed in neatly pressed thobe. His initial presence gives off wisdom and humility. "As-salamu alaykum," he states.

"Wa àlaykumu s-salāmu wa rahmatu l-lāhi wa barakātuh," replies Keith.

Hugging and gently pressing shoulder to shoulder, the two men shake hands and follow with a kiss on the cheek. Veronica smiles and places her hand toward the gentleman as if she expects a handshake. The gentleman looks at her and simply smiles before he gestures to Keith. "Excuse me. Will it be OK If talk to you briefly in private?" he asks.

"Yes!" Keith replies. "Excuse me darling. I will be right back."

They only take a few steps, but they are far enough so that Veronica won't be able to hear the conversation. Quietly she stands there with Zacori by her side, trying to figure out the conversation through their body movements. Whatever is being said, it gives her the impression that he is explaining something to Keith, who pays very close attention and only nods yes as the gentleman politely speaks.

I wonder what is going on over there. Are they not going to welcome him into the mosque? Is it because he is African? They'd better not even try it, or I will give them a piece of my mind today, she thinks to herself before noticing Keith walking back over. "Is everything OK?" she asks.

"Well, yes and no. He was just explaining some of the rules of the mosque to me. The first thing is that he meant no disrespect in not shaking your hand. In the Islamic religion a man is not allowed to touch another man's woman, so that is the reason he only smiled when saying hello instead of shaking your hand. The second thing is that in the house of worship and in public you must cover your head." He pulls a cloth from his pocket. Before Veronica can even respond, Keith begins to place the garment over her head.

"Please, honey. We will talk about it later, but I really need you to do this for me right now," he says.

"Well, at least let me fix it my way! I understand the reasoning behind the garment, and I knew that if I decided to enter this house of worship I would have to abide by the rules, so I am cool with it. I do watch TV, you know," Veronica says, smiling while fixing the garment over her head properly.

Keith clutches her hand as they proceed down the hallway of the mosque. Veronica is amazed by the structure and design of the place. It almost gives her the feeling of being in an actual Middle Eastern house of worship. The aroma of frankincense fills the air, and shoes are in a perfectly parallel line near where people wash their feet and hands. The majority of the women stand along the wall, and occasionally Veronica can hear them speak in their native languages, unsure if they are actually talking about her. She can see their eyes glancing toward her and then looking down at Zacori. Feeling a little insecure about things, she brings

Zacori a little closer to her side. Not only are the women curious of the little blue-eyed kid in their mosque, but the men also begin to wonder. Another gentleman approaches Keith as he stands amongst the new brothers of his mosque.

"I'm sorry, brother. If you don't mind, can I have a few words with you over here?" the gentleman asks. They take a few steps to a small area located in the rear of the mosque. "I don't know if you were informed, but we don't allow children in this mosque. If you want, we have a separate place designated for them to practice prayer and learn the correct ways of Islam," he says, smiling at Keith.

"It's actually our first time here. A friend of mine recommended this mosque to us, and my fiancée has just decided to convert to Islam, so some of the rules are still new to us. You can believe the mistake will not be made again," says Keith.

"I see. You will be welcomed with open arms, I assure you. Your choice in faith is wise. Is this your child?" he says looking toward Zacori.

"No!" Keith quickly responds. "He is the child that my fiancée cares for. We didn't want to miss prayer, so she brought him along."

"So she is a nanny of some sort?"

"Yes. Exactly. Before we met, she was looking after children for income, but now that we are spiritually and emotionally connected, things will change for the better."

"You seem to be a good man with great intentions. Come! I will introduce you to some of the other brothers," the man says.

The two begin to walk off, with Keith totally ignoring that he left Veronica and Zacori standing alone. Veronica doesn't really pay too much attention, as she is still caught up in admiring the mosque. *This may not be that bad,* she thinks to herself.

Suddenly a voice speaking in Arabic echoes throughout the mosque, bringing to attention all the men, who head toward the main floor. One by one, they take off their shoes and form parallel lines next to one another on their knees. As they listen to the words of the Imam, worshipers periodically place their heads on the floor, bowing down in respect and submission to God. It is amazing to Veronica to witness for the first time the discipline in their rituals of prayer. It is far from the practices of Christianity and Baptist churches she has visited in the past, but Veronica knows she has to do more research before making a final decision.

After prayer, a small meet and greet is held in the lower level of the mosque for all the people who are there for the first time. A fairly young Middle Eastern woman approaches Veronica as she stands with Zacori and introduces herself.

"Hi. My name is Mya, and your name is?"

"Veronica. It's a pleasure to meet you too," she says, feeling happy that she has finally been approached by a woman who seems to be generally pleasant.

"And who is this darling little boy?" Mya asks, kneeling down and running her hands gently through Zacori's hair. Holding onto Veronica's leg, Zacori looks toward the ground and remains silent.

"His name is Zacori. Say hello, Zacori. It's OK," Veronica says, urging him on.

"What a nice-looking little boy," Mya says. "He looks very well taken care of. How much do you actually charge per day?"

Veronica pauses with a strange look upon her face. "Charge for what?"

"I'm sorry. Where are my manners? This really isn't the proper place to discuss what you do for a living, but when we heard how good of a nanny you are, I just wanted to take advantage of the opportunity," says Mya.

"Wow! Let's start all over," Veronica says, shocked. What has led you to believe that I am a nanny?"

"Your fiancé. It's really nothing to be ashamed of. The fact that you brought your boss' child here to the mosque to make prayer shows great character on your behalf."

As Veronica stands there quietly, she analyzes every word coming from the mouth of this woman who is obviously misled. It takes every ounce of her strength to remain calm and not react. Deep down she knows she has to remain a lady, not just for her own image, but also to not ruin Keith's chances of being accepted.

"Excuse me. I am sorry that you were misinformed of the true relationship between this child and me. This is actually my son, not by birth, but by love. When his parents were unfortunately unable to care for him anymore, I promised his mother that I would do everything in my power to help her son one day become the man his father failed to be. He is with me because I could not watch him be placed into a foster care system that has failed so many kids before him. Tomorrow morning when I take him to his private school, I will gladly ask one of the nannies who drops off other people's kids if they know of any help. OK?"

"Thank you so much. I would really appreciate that. Here is my number, and I am sorry for the misunderstanding once again," Mya says.

"No problem!" Veronica says smiling. Once Mya has walked away, she pauses for a moment before walking out of the front door. She looks toward Keith, who is talking to a group of men over to the side. He glances at her but remains talking as she walks out. Once at the door, Veronica quickly grabs the cloth covering her head and throws it to the floor before exiting.

⟨⟩

A few hours have passed before Keith arrives at the apartment. Infuriated by what happened earlier, Veronica sits on the couch reading a book quietly as Keith sits down besides her. Ignoring that he's even there, she obviously doesn't want to be bothered. Staring at Veronica without saying a word as if nothing ever happened, Keith knows eventually she'll break if he looks at her long enough. If there is anything Keith is good at, it's making her laugh no matter what is going on.

"Hey!" he says, tapping her on the leg. Once he realizes she is really upset and tapping her won't work, he blows air into her face as forcefully as he can until he becomes winded and the air is a simple whistle. As he catches his breath and starts over, Veronica puts her hand up to block the air and softly smiles behind the book when Keith begins to cough. She quickly takes her pillow and tosses it into his face, which causes him to curl up on the couch.

"I can't believe you! How could you have embarrassed me like that in front of complete strangers?"

"If you didn't like the color of the hijab, all you had to do was say so. I would have gladly grabbed you another one," Keith states, attempting to break the ice.

"I am laughing, but I really don't find this funny. How could you have the audacity to lead these people to believe that I was some sort of nanny? Do you understand how embarrassed I was when this woman approached me asking how much I charge? The only reason I kept my composure is the fact that I am a lady first at all times. Second, no one will bring me to embarrassing you or Zacori in public. This is my family, but I want you to always remember this. I can be the sweetest person in the world, but if you ever take my kindness for weakness or lead anyone to believe I am a servant, I will walk out this door with my boy and never return to you or this house."

"I'm sorry, but I didn't know what to say when they began to ask me about Zacori. I was stuck, and the first thing that came to my head was that you're his nanny. It just seemed believable," says Keith.

"You should have told them the truth. I'm not embarrassed when I walk down the street with him because I know the truth. I was more than willing to stand up and take responsibility for him after his fabric-pushing pimp of a father was imprisoned and his mother killed herself in fear that she would be poor again. He is my son. That's what you should have told him. As a matter of fact, the first words out of your mouth should have been 'That's my fiancée and her son.' Of course it's different. Nobody judges or has an opinion when you see white people adopting little black children or famous actors and actresses going all over the world adopting children of color like a new bag or the latest trend. So you know what, I guess I am the opposite because I have one of theirs."

Keith is speechless as he suddenly realizes how deeply Veronica feels about Zacori. Her words are full of truth and compassion. "I don't know what to say right now, and sorry just won't be enough. I realize that I didn't take your feelings into consideration, and I definitely didn't think before I spoke. All I can ask is that you forgive me for my ignorance."

"I will forgive you, only because I love you and believe in you. The only thing I want you to understand is that Zacori is just as much a part of my life as you are, and we are one. It's beautiful to become deeply involved in religion, and I will support you and stand next to you as you travel through this journey in life. But you must respect and acknowledge the fact that I am taking care of a child who is not from our loins but will always be in my life."

"I promise to not only accept that, but to respect you first always and raise him as if he were my own," Keith says, leaning closer in to gently kiss her lips as she embraces him with a hug.

Chapter 12

It has been two years now that Keith and Veronica have been married. Zacori is now eight and has become a very well mannered young man. As a family they have involved themselves more in the practices and culture of Islam with Zacori adapting especially quickly to the change. He has learned most of the prayers and looks forward to attending the mosque on weekends for youth services.

Today is the first day he will be attending his new school, and Veronica is so proud to see him flourish on his own. Keith has been an amazing stepfather to Zacori. He has really stepped up and taken on the responsibility of caring for and helping to raise Zacori as his own son. They have become inseparable. From prayer to long talks at night, together Keith and Zacori spend quality time with each other like father and son. Many days Veronica observes their interactions hoping one day she'll be able to have a child of her own, but for now it's all about Zacori.

Zacori begins walking into the schoolyard when he suddenly turns toward Veronica, who is waving goodbye with all the other parents. He runs up to her as fast as he can with his backpack swaying so hard he almost loses his balance and grabs her around the waist, squeezing her as tightly as he can.

"It's OK. You're a big boy now," she tells him, rubbing his silky blond hair.

"I know. I just wanted to tell you that I love you, Mom!" he says before running back toward the other kids. Shocked by the words that have just come from his mouth, Veronica realizes the impact that she has had on his life. It gives her a feeling she has never felt before, one of warmth and being needed. She stands for a few minutes smiling as she watches Zacori in line with the rest of the students.

"I love you too," she whispers.

As Zacori stands under the sign of his new classroom, Veronica walks over and to meet the teacher like the other parents when the security officer suddenly approaches her. "Excuse me, miss, is it possible that I can have a word with you over here to the side?"

"Sure," she responds.

As they walk over, Veronica begins to notice the other parents looking and whispering to one another. She even sees some of the parents shaking their heads as they whisper.

"I don't mean to bother you, but it has become school policy that we randomly search baggage as people enter the school. Please don't be offended. After 9/11 you can never be too careful. If you don't mind, could you please open your bag for me?"

"I've never heard of this being done inside a school, but if it's the policy I have no objections," she says before opening the bag.

The security officer briefly flashes a light into the bag, looking for anything suspicious. It suddenly comes to Veronica; she hears one father whisper, "You can never be too safe these days. They'll do anything," as he looks on.

Veronica realizes it is could merely her hijab that has caused people to be alarmed. As this is a predominately white school located on the Upper West Side, some negative stereotypes and media-influenced ignorance may be major factors in their obvious prejudices. Being the type of person to never feed into ignorance, Veronica simply smiles at the officer, patiently waiting for him to finish.

"I just want to applaud you for doing such a good job. The world is such a crazy place, and you are playing a big part in keeping our children safe," she says.

"I'm just doing my job. Thank you for being so understanding. It looks like everything is good to go here. Enjoy the rest of your day," he says.

Her initial intentions are to report the officer's actions to the principal, but deep down she knows it will only cause problems in the future for Zacori. His education is more important than her personal feelings at the moment, so she decides to exit the school without saying a word. It saddens her to know that people can be so cruel and thoughtless to others strictly because of race and religious beliefs. After converting to Islam, she realizes this is only the beginning. *How do the other Muslim women feel? Do they go through this on a daily basis?*

Though Veronica has only recently begun to wear her hijab, she has already begun to feel the prejudices against Muslim people, especially women who must be covered in public. Fearful of what people may think, Veronica decides to remove her headscarf before she gets on the train to go to the appointment with the fertility doctor recommended by her gynecologist. Today is not only big for Zacori; it is also special for her. Today she will find out if she will ever be able to have children. Deep in her heart she desperately wants to have a child with Keith to make things complete. Keith has done such a good job with Zacori and supported her during terrible times that she feels he deserves to have a child of his own.

It's 10:20 a.m. when Veronica arrives at the fertility doctor's office. After registering with the receptionist, she patiently waits for her name to be called. There are only a few women in the office today. She decides to put her hijab back on since she is in the presence of men in a closed area. Sitting adjacent to her in the waiting area is a young married couple holding hands while the husband rubs his wife's belly. Veronica can't help but to look, finding the two of them extremely supportive and comforting to one another. She smiles at them, wishing Keith were with her.

"Veronica!" the receptionist yells.

"Yes!" she quickly responds, making her way to the office door. She crosses her fingers; preparing herself for whatever news she is about to hear. As she sits in the office, the doctor remains silent as he looks over her chart, fumbling from page to page without saying a word. Tapping her fingers and looking at the ceiling, Veronica can't wait any longer.

"OK, doc, you're killing me with suspense!" she says, laughing. "Please, just tell me already."

"Well, I am looking over the results from your fertility test, and to be honest with you I really don't see anything stopping you from getting pregnant. I do have a series of questions to ask you before we move on," the doctor says.

"Sure," Veronica responds.

"I know that you don't have any children, but how about your husband?"

"No. This will also be his first. Actually it will be our first. I do have a son, but it's complicated."

"Really? I didn't see that in the documentation sent by your previous gynecologist," the doctor says. Veronica reaches into her purse and proudly pulls a picture of Zacori out of her wallet.

"Wow! What a handsome little guy. You said this is your son?" the doctor asks, looking down at the picture.

"Yes and no. He's not my biological son, but I am raising him while his parents are away, so he is kind of my son," Veronica responds.

"Well, he is absolutely adorable."

"Thanks!"

"After looking over your labs and the test we performed, I am very confident in telling you everything is fine. My only suggestion is that your husband sees an urologist to check his sperm count to see if there is a problem there. But to really be honest with you, timing and patience are major contributing factors in becoming pregnant. Take this cup home. The instructions are on the handout inside the baggie. In three days, just return the specimen to the nearest lab listed on the paper and we will go from there, OK? Let's hope for the best," says Dr. Zimmerman.

The two share eager smiles before standing. "Thank you so much for all you've done. I truly appreciate it. See you in a few weeks at the follow-up appointment," Veronica says.

"I realize you are wearing a head wrap today. Are you cold, or is it for religion?" Dr. Zimmerman asks.

"Oh, you have never seen me wearing my hijab. I have recently converted to my husband's religion, Islam. I usually wear it in the presence of men or outside, but lately I feel that people are quick to judge me negatively when I am in public. It may sound crazy but…"

"I totally understand. Remember, I too am from the Middle East, and my wife constantly tells me of the ridiculous comments she hears. I will tell you like I tell her: people fear the unknown, and as long as anyone disguises himself or herself, they will never be accepted as who they are. So, never be ashamed of who you are," he says.

"Thank you, doctor. Thanks for all you've done, along with the great advice. I will be seeing you soon," says Veronica before exiting.

Once Veronica leaves the office, Dr. Zimmerman calls the front desk.

"Yes, Dr. Zimmerman?" the receptionist answers.

"Has the young lady I just saw left the office as of yet?"

"Yes, I just informed her to call for her next appointment. Is there a problem?"

"No, no problem. I just don't think I will be taking care of her moving forward. When she calls, just inform her that I am really busy and refer her to Dr. Ahad's office," he says.

"Sure, no problem," she responds before hanging up.

Dr. Zimmerman sits at his desk looking over Veronica's chart before tossing it into the trash next to his desk. "Muslims," he says before moving on to the next chart without any remorse for his actions.

Later that evening, Veronica tries to find a way to explain her doctor's visit to Keith without offending him. It is routine that the family eats together at the table before the evening prayer, so she feels that the best time to sit Keith down and explain what the doctor has requested is after Zacori has already fallen asleep and things have settled down. Veronica expresses that she has something really important to discuss.

Once Keith realizes the concern in her voice, he decides to sit with her immediately. "What's going on? Is everything OK with you?" he asks.

"Everything is fine. I just wanted to sit down with you privately and discuss some of the things that happened when I visited Dr. Zimmerman, a fertility doctor, today."

"You went to a fertility doctor? Today?" Keith asks before taking a deep breath and slouching down into the couch.

"Yes. I know I didn't discuss this with you first, but I just wanted to know why I haven't been able to get pregnant after all this time. I truly wanted to make sure that there was nothing wrong with me," she says.

"I don't understand why you felt the need to do that. We already have a child, Zacori. Plus, I don't know if a child is exactly what we are ready for at this time. Why would you not discuss this with me first?" He sits upright on the couch. "And what did this doctor have to say?"

"Everything has come back great so far with my physical, so he wants…"

Keith quickly sits up from his position and interrupts, asking "He?" in an aggressive tone.

Veronica pauses for a moment, feeling fear once she hears the anger in his voice. Becoming more agitated, Keith chuckles, looking toward the ground and shaking his head in disbelief. "And what is it that your 'doctor' has come up with, that you're not the problem? Let me guess! Is it an assumption that I am the problem? Are these the words this man has chosen for you to tell me?" He stands in rage. "That I am less of a man and he wants to study my manhood? Tell me! Is this what this Jew has suggested to my wife about me?"

"He only said that if you can give a sperm sample it may..."

A thunderous blow to the face, which causes her to lose consciousness for a few seconds, suddenly strikes Veronica. She can only hear the far-away echo of Keith's voice as she tries to get herself back to normal. *Oh, God!* She thinks to herself before feeling warm fluid coming from her nose. Wiping her nose with her hand, she trembles in fear at the sight of her own blood. She shields herself to block any further abuse from Keith before looking into his eyes in the midst of his rage.

Realizing what he has done, Keith falls to his knees pleading for forgiveness once he sees the blood coming from her face. "I'm so sorry!" he repeats, attempting to bring Veronica close to him. She finally gives in, only to not receive another blow from him.

"I can't believe that you just hit me," she says, looking at the blood on her hand and holding her nose. She grabs a cloth from the table to apply pressure. "Oh God! This is not happening."

Keith makes every attempt to try and console her, but his efforts are only met with resistance as Veronica refuses to let him hold her. "I am sorry, my love. Words cannot begin to tell you how much I am. My anger got the best of me when I felt that you betrayed me. There is no excuse for what I have just done, but I promise it will never happen again. Please, Veronica! Please forgive me," he pleads. He kisses her cheek and places his fingers on her chin to be eye to eye as he apologizes.

In this moment Veronica wants to run out the door as fast as she can, but she doesn't. Instead she sits there and listens to the lies until they become believable. She thinks about where she will go and what she will do if she leaves. How will she be able to support Zacori and pay for his schooling without Keith? What will her parents think of her? All these things run through her mind as she listens to Keith excuse his actions, but more than anything she wants to believe him, and her heart tells her to forgive him. So she stays.

It was the first of many times that Keith would put his hands on Veronica, only to apologize for losing his temper later. She has now begun to walk in public with a burqa to disguise the abuse. She is alone and scared. There is no one to turn to or money to leave, so she accepts the treatment of the man she once loved. The periodic abuse has even begun to affect Zacori. Once a quiet child, he has now turned into a rebellious ten-year-old, acting out in school and verbally disrespecting others. Veronica knows this is the result of witnessing violence in the household, and something needs to be done.

The man who once saved her from a brutal rape has now become the same savage he protected her from or worse, hiding under the title of a husband. The lovemaking that was so passionately shared has become emotionless, rough, meaningless sex. *How many women are in my shoes?* She thinks to herself. How many women disguise pain through smiles and hide bruises with expensive makeup? It puzzles her to think of what happens to a man emotionally when he realizes he no longer loves his woman. The only excuse she can come up with is that this behavior is acceptable to the elder men in the mosque, the men whom Keith has begun visiting more frequently and who mentor him under the umbrella of religion. The men who force their women to walk behind them in public and keep them from the outside so long they develop bone deficiency from lack of sunlight. But she finds all these things hard to believe, knowing Islam is enriched with teachings of respect for all men and women.

Veronica needs a plan, and she needs it fast. She searches the apartment desperately for the extra cash Keith sometimes keeps around the house. Grabbing a small bag to fill with cash and clothes, she falls to her knees in tears, exhausted staring at the ceiling.

"WHY? Why is this happening?" she screams. "Linda, I am so sorry I failed you. I tried sister. God knows I had the best intentions to do the right thing for him, but I am weak from the same poison that caused you to no longer breathe. Is Keith on a path of destruction that will one day end my life, or will I beat him to it? Some say the dead can listen but cry with no response. I know I am asking for something impossible, but for the sake and sanity of our little boy, please take me away from this hell," she says. *Oh what am I doing*, she thinks to herself. *I must be foolish praying to what obviously doesn't exist.* Whimpering in sorrow on the floor, she suddenly remembers something that Linda once said to her:

"Even when my heart pumped and my lungs breathed air, it only travelled to a hollow shell. The weaker the heart becomes, the emptier the soul gets."

Sitting on the floor for a few minutes, Veronica decides she has had enough. No longer will she be a weak woman afraid of facing life and overcoming abuse. She takes off her burqa and walks toward the mirror on the dresser to take a good look at herself. Staring deep into the eyes of the woman in front of her, she begins to reconnect with her soul.

Chapter 13

Seven years have passed since the tragic death of Linda and incarceration of Mr. Burns. At times it seems the absence of Zacori's biological parents doesn't have a negative impact on him. He continues to call Veronica Mom and never mentions that he notices the color difference. Her relationship with Keith hasn't changed very much. He continues to provide for his family, but the fact that they don't have a child together causes distance between them, which she believes is the true reason for the periodic abuse these days.

Keith constantly has the elder men over, and she hears the men talking about the worthlessness of a woman if she is unable to bear kids. It doesn't affect Veronica today, as it would have in the past. At this rate, she would rather have an abortion than bring another child into her world of chaos. She knows the man that she once loved more than life itself has secrets, but she remains humble and loyal to the vows she made before God when they married.

In some ways she almost feels like Linda, trapped by the thought of being poor again and living a nightmare with a man who mistreats her. The only difference is, unlike Linda, she suffers physical and mental abuse from her husband. These days she is forced to wear her hijab in public, especially when dropping Zacori to school. If the school is to ever find out the truth about what is going on in the house, they wouldn't hesitate to call Child Protective Services for an investigation, so she hides her identity behind the hijab and looks at the world through the abaya.

For the second time in her life she is alone. The relationship with her parents has diminished, as they look at Keith as their financial savior, the person who helps without hesitation when they ask him to send money to help them out of poverty. They would rather turn the other cheek than protect the daughter that once counted her pennies to send home. Keith has even been able to convince her parents to send her sister to school abroad, of course at his expense. All she has are Zacori and her promise to keep him safe until he can be on his own. Even through the dark times, the only light is those big blue eyes she fell in love with the first time they stared at her in the coffee shop years ago.

He makes things complete in her puzzling world. He is an honor student, with some of the best middle schools in the city being great prospects due to his grades. His father was one of the best businessmen in the city with recognition among corporate America. From time to time, she would receive mail from Mr. Burns asking about Zacori, but once Keith said there should be no more communication, the letters never came again.

It's three o'clock, time for Veronica to pick Zacori up from school. He hates when she is late. Every day after school she picks him up and walks through Bryant Park, close to the coffee shop where it all began. Of course Zacori doesn't remember, but to Veronica it is a place to reflect on a time of peace and prosperity in her life. Every day she sits quietly on the bench observing the people talking and children playing. She sometimes closes her eyes, allowing her mind to run freely to another place.

"Mom! Mom!" Zacori's voice echoes.

"Yes," she responds.

"Can I ask you a question? Two questions actually," he asks excitedly.

"Sure. Of course you can."

"Can I have a party for my birthday?"

"A party? Let me see if that's something I can do first," she says, knowing how Keith may feel about this. "And your second question?"

"Well, some of the kids at school ask me sometimes why we're different colors, and the teachers say you're my nanny. I know you're my mom, but are you my nanny also? And what's a nanny?"

Veronica hesitates for a moment, thrown off by the very question she knew he would one day ask. She doesn't know if he can handle the truth about his parents. She grabs his hands and tries to explain the best she can. "We are all humans. The only thing that truly matters in life is what's in here," she says, pointing her finger to his heart. "A parent is a person who loves and cares genuinely for their child, no matter the circumstances, and a nanny is a person whose job it is to help parents with day-to-day activities they just may not have time to do. Sometimes parents have enough faith in that person that the nanny becomes just like a parent. I'm both. There's only one thing different."

"What's that?" he asks.

"I don't get paid for loving you so much," Veronica jokingly says before grabbing Zacori and tickling his belly. "Come on! Let's go by the coffee shop and grab something to drink. Thirsty?"

"A little," he responds.

As they proceed through the park hand in hand, Veronica can't help but to feel people looking at them. She knows why they look and stare. She even overhears one man say to his friend after they pass, "Look at this. Now the terrorists get to watch our children." Entering the coffee shop doesn't stop the ignorance from following her. Veronica knows wearing her abaya in public will bring her some negative attention, but the bruises will only bring her more.

As she and Zacori stand patiently in line waiting to be served, she realizes the cashiers are calling to other patrons first, even if they've come in behind her. Only when the cashier has no choice does she finally acknowledge and call them to the counter. "Yes?" she says without giving Veronica eye contact.

"I'm fine and yourself?" Veronica responds sarcastically. Annoyed by the rude behavior of the waitress, she can't help but to comment. "It's very polite and customer service-savvy to at least greet your patrons with eye contact when they are supporting your business."

"Well, most of my patrons I can actually see," the cashier responds. It feels as though time stands still inside in the small café. Both of the ladies stand in total silence awaiting a response from the next. Veronica is furious with rage. The unnecessary comments have taken her to a place of anger that she's never felt before. She balls up her fist, clutching her bottom lip with her teeth. Her scalp becomes moist with sweat. They ladies size each other up like cowboys in a saloon shootout.

"You know what, I should really…" Veronica begins to say before a tugging on her sleeve disrupts her.

"Mom. Mom, let's go," Zacori's voice says before releasing her mind from the rage she wants to express.

"Of course!"

Veronica looks the young cashier in the eyes before she exits the café. The cashier throws her apron on the counter furiously and mumbles, "They have some nerve," before exiting to a back room.

Later that evening after prayer, Keith expresses the importance of an upcoming trip to Nigeria that he will be taking within the next few days. He tells Veronica that upon his return, things will be different for the family. It's the same story she is all too familiar with, but he assures her there will be more structure in the house and he will be giving her more help. As Veronica listens, her heart once again takes his words serious. Like many other people in abusive relationships, she is searching for peace and calmness in her life.

But for now, nothing makes her happier than when Keith is away. It gives her and Zacori time to rest and enjoy each other without anyone around. The physical abuse has calmed down, but the verbal abuse has taken its place. She would rather be hit than told she is nothing. Nothing is what she feels she's become in every aspect of her life. She searches desperately to find a way to make herself feel whole again, trying numerous hobbies, from knitting to painting. Even involving herself in the mosque more is an option, but she finds that the women there are no better than those who stereotype her in the street. They look down on her, still thinking she is nothing more than a nanny who cares for white children. Her life is a secret that if ever told can take away her only reason for existence.

It's coming up on Zacori's birthday soon, and while Keith is away Veronica thinks it would be a good idea to have a small party for him. He doesn't have many friends that she knows of, but between the kids at school and a certain few from the mosque, he is bound to have a good time. The only problem she faces is Keith's approval, but this is for Zacori. If it means having an argument with Keith or whatever else it brings, then so be it.

Her finances are limited. Living with only the necessities is a new theory Keith has adopted from the elder men in the mosque, while at the same time giving them large contributions for the restructuring of the mosque. She knows it isn't a good idea, but what can she do? It's his money, and no matter what they go through personally, he always puts Zacori's education and well being first. Of course it helps that she stumbled upon the cash he keeps in the house a short time ago.

As she sits down to prepare the list of people to invite, she pauses for a minute to reminisce on the last few years they have had together. *Wow! He is going to be 11 already*, she thinks to herself. If only Linda were here to see him grow into a young man, she would be so proud. "Linda, I thought you were being selfish in taking your life, but in fact you gave me something to live for." She shakes her head, smiling as she continues the guest list for the party.

Chapter 14

The time has finally come for Zacori's birthday party, and the house is decorated with his favorite skateboard characters. Veronica has prepared dishes that will accommodate many diets so no one feels left out. There is a pretty mixed group of children, with some kids from his school and the rest from the mosque. The kids are having a great time, but the diversity of the parents can't be ignored. All the parents of the Muslim kids stay strictly to themselves on one side of the room while the rest of the parents mingle amongst one another, making small conversation and attempting to have a good time.

Some of the school kids' parents have asked for Zacori's parents, eager to finally meet them, but Veronica remains with her story that unfortunately they are out of the country. Despite some of the religious beliefs and opinions of others, Veronica attempts to appease everyone while visiting her home. She plays music for the children to dance and enjoy themselves. As the day goes on, the party becomes a huge success and things loosen up a little. Even some of the Muslim parents briefly dance and laugh with the children. It makes her feel good to see everyone having a good time with one another, and most of all, to see Zacori's joy at having all his friends in one place for him.

The party has come to an end with the last of the guests finally leaving. Veronica walks the final couple to the door and then back into the living area, where Zacori waits by the table, eating the last of the potato chips in the bowl.

"Did you have a good time?" she asks.

"It was great, Mom. Thank you! Thank you!" he repeats, wrapping his arms around her neck as tightly as he can.

She rubs his head and gently kisses his candy-covered cheeks. "I'm glad you enjoyed yourself, but it is time for you to take a bath and head to bed." She pats him on the backside and points in the direction of the bathroom.

Zacori turns and runs toward the bathroom before stopping suddenly, running back to Veronica and hugging her again. "I love you so much, Mom. You're the greatest mom in the world."

"I love you too," Veronica responds, her voice cracking with emotion. "This doesn't mean you're excluded from helping to clean up before your shower, young man."

An hour has passed when Veronica re-enters the living room, which was left quite a mess. She decides to lie down on the couch and get some rest before cleaning up. With no knowledge of how long she was asleep, Veronica is startled awake by the slamming of a door. She looks around the room still in a daze and calls to Zacori, but there is no answer until she is startled by the voice of a man.

"What is this mess in my home? What has happened here?" The voice begins to elevate. "Did I give you permission to have a party in my house?"

Veronica's stomach begins to tighten up with fear, almost causing her to urinate on herself. She now realizes that Keith has returned from his trip. "Turn and face me when I speak to you!" he shouts.

Turning to face him, Veronica trembles with fear before being met with a forceful blow to the face, which causes her to fall to her hands and knees, dazed with blood pooling in the palm of her hand. Hearing the blunt force hitting her body and seeing flashes of light as her face is struck, she lies hopeless as she is savagely beaten. Through it all, she moans in pain from each crushing blow and kick Keith applies to her body until she looks up and sees Zacori in the doorway of his room crying, witness-ing Keith in the midst of his abuse. She reaches toward him as if she needs him to rescue her. It is a reach for mercy, one of sur-render. She begins to crawl toward Zacori but is too weak to tell him to run.

Veronica's attempt to reach for Zacori catches Keith's atten-tion, so he begins to walk toward the bedroom in which Zacori stands. Grabbing Zacori by the neck of his pajamas, Keith drags him into the bedroom as Veronica finds enough energy to scream "ALLAH, PLEASE! Allah, please help us!" Exhausted from the beating, her eyes become heavy and her breaths shorter as she lies on the floor. She attempts to rise, only to lose her footing and hit her head on the coffee table.

The next morning, she awakens in the same spot she fell. She gen-tly touches her face and jumps up, confused initially about her whereabouts. "Zacori? Zacori!" she screams, but there is no answer.

"He is already at school. I took him this morning," Keith says from the living room, blankly staring straight ahead at the wall in front of him.

"Is he OK?" she nervously asks.

"If you think I would hurt the child, you're wrong. I may not know who I am anymore, but I will never hurt a child of God," he says.

"Am I not a child of God?" Veronica asks

"You are the property of man," Keith answers, never looking in her direction.

Veronica remains still on the floor, afraid to move not know-ing what Keith's actions will be. He whispers, gently rubbing his prayer beads between his fingers. The room is quiet and cold as Veronica eases her way to her feet and walks to the bathroom. Keith never looks her way or stops praying until the bathroom door slams and locks.

Chapter 15

A few days have passed when Veronica decides it's time to begin to pick up the pieces after Keith's brutal assault. Her face is still healing, but air is what she needs to begin the healing process mentally. Deciding to go for afternoon prayer, she knows at least she can find a corner and just be alone with God. Once afternoon prayer is over, she returns home to pick Zacori up from school. It's been a week since she's done this, so she wants to freshen up and grab a few dollars so they can visit the coffee shop they frequent.

Upon entering the house, Veronica can hear Keith in the kitchen. It isn't out of the ordinary for him to have an elder come over after prayer, so she thinks nothing of it at first. Entering the doorway of the kitchen, she sees a young fair-skinned woman sitting next to him before looking up and gesturing to Keith that they are no longer alone. He turns to see Veronica before introducing the two.

"Veronica, this is Fatima. Fatima, this is Veronica."

"As-salamu alaykum, sister," says Fatima.

"Wa alaykumu s-salam" Veronica responds, nodding her head in peaceful greeting. She looks at the way Keith looks at Fatima and becomes very uneasy with this young woman being in her house. "Can I fix you something, sister?"

Fatima looks at Keith, awaiting his response before she answers Veronica.

"No, she's fine." Keith responds. "Fatima is going to be staying here to help with things around the house, and – how can I say this? Be family for the two of us," he says, passionately grabbing Fatima's hands.

Veronica observes immediately that her husband has welcomed another wife into the household. *Was this why there was urgency to travel to Africa so much?* She asks herself. Veronica attempts to recall Fatima's face to remember if she's seen her before in the mosque, but she knows they have never met. Veronica is unable to have children and she knows Keith would use that as his excuse to marry another woman, one much younger and more fertile. After all the struggles and abuse Veronica has gone through with Keith, adultery crosses the line. There is no way she is going to knowingly share her bed with another woman and her husband, but she remains humble and smiles.

"Well, it was nice meeting you. Welcome to our home. Please help yourself to anything you may need. If you can excuse me, I will leave you to continue your conversation," she says.

Exiting to the back bedroom to take off her burqa in front of the mirror, she thinks of all the pain and suffering she has been through in her life, including the attempted rape and brutal beatings since she hasn't been able to produce children. Quietly she locks the door and heads toward the bed, kneeling down to her knees to pray as she did when she practiced Christianity. If anyone can help straighten her life out now, Veronica can only believe it is Jesus. She closes her eyes to pray, but is unable to as she is interrupted by feelings of violence and rage building up inside her.

She looks up to the sky and says, "You know my heart," before coming to her feet and going to the closet. She removes some of her regular clothing and quickly places it in a bag. Scrambling around, she comes across a small box tucked away in the corner of the closet and opens it, finding some cash inside. It isn't much, but it's better than nothing. It is time for the abuse to end. It is time for the embarrassing facial wounds forcing her to hide behind religious clothes to end. She is a woman scorned, abused and fed up. She refuses to suffer any longer from emotional misery or take the same route of her friend Linda. She can no longer ignore that she is married to an evil animal.

If it is the presence of another woman that has finally woke Veronica up, then it is a good enough reason for her to go. She knows why Fatima is here, and her spirit speaks to her. To do things immaturely won't produce a positive outcome. Zacori still needs to go to the best schools and be provided for properly. Keith may not respect that he is still legally married, but those vows still mean something to her.

She sits for a few minutes thinking of what is best and what kind of advice she would give herself. The money that she's grabbed is a fair amount, but she knows it won't be enough to live in New York City, taking into consideration Zacori's school and other needs. It is time to go, and that is the only solution. She wraps her head before leaving the room leaving her keys on the dresser and making her way to the kitchen.

Passing by the kitchen, Veronica pauses as she vividly hears the conversation between Keith and the young woman. She takes shallow breaths to keep calm as she walks by, witnessing Keith with his arm now resting upon Fatima's shoulder, gently massaging it. She remains calm, holding her head down.

"I am going to the market to pick up a few items. Is there anything that you will need?" she asks.

"No, we're fine. But there is no need for you to rush back. We'll just be catching up on a few things while you're gone," Keith says.

"Sure. Hope everything works to your liking," Veronica sarcastically remarks.

Fatima nods without saying a word, only making brief eye contact with Veronica as she walks toward the front door. Veronica mumbles, "God be with you," as she exits. She rests her head against the door, taking a deep breath before finally leaving. She realizes Keith was so into Fatima he didn't notice the bag on her back. Betrayed by this man in every way possible, she throws her hijab to the floor, stepping on it to signify the end of her marriage and ties to Islam.

Three o'clock arrives, and it's time to pick Zacori up from school. She stands in the corridor as she does every day, waiting for his class to come downstairs. It's the first time in a long time Veronica has come to Zacori's school completely uncovered, exposed to the world as who she truly is. A few of the parents look at her strangely without commenting, and she thinks it's because of the bruising on her face from Keith's last attack, but it doesn't matter what people say or think. Veronica is standing with her head high and feeling no shame for the way she looks. She is approached by one of the teacher's aides she's seen in the past, but she doesn't recognize her without the burqa.

"Hi. Is there something I can help you with?"

"No, I am actually here to pick up my son," Veronica replies.

"Your son?" the aide asks, curiously looking at Veronica's face. "I don't believe we've ever met before. Are you sure you're in the right school?"

"Yes, I am sure. I have picked him up every day for the last two years from this same spot, and if…" Veronica, realizing that her voice has begun to echo into the halls, stops to regain her composure. "I'm sorry. I have to remember that a lot of people are not accustomed to seeing me outside of my religious garments. I am here to pick up Zacori Burns," she says.

"Oh, I know him," the aide states. "You said your son and it threw me off a little bit. I always thought you were the nanny. Correct?"

"Did I say son? We are so close it seems that he is my son at times. I am sorry if I misled you," Veronica quickly responds.

"No, it's fine. Believe me, I understand. To be honest with you, a family that I was a nanny for helped me to get the job here actually. I totally understand how close you can get to the kids," says the aide.

The two ladies pause for a moment. Veronica begins to notice more and more how the young woman can't help looking at her face. She tries to cover her cheeks as much as she can with her hair, but it is of no help.

"Don't worry, he's nice sometimes," Veronica says, trying to make a joke of her appearance.

"I'm sorry. It's just..." the teacher's assistant begins to explain before being interrupted by Veronica.

"I know how the bruises may look, but... I just can't anymore..." Veronica tries to finish her sentence but the words are broken up by cries. She takes a deep breath and continues to look straight ahead, regaining her composure.

"Do you have a few minutes? Maybe we can talk," the assistant says, clutching Veronica's hand to assure her everything is fine.

"No, no, I'll be fine."

"I know you will. But I needed someone at a time in my life too, sister. I've worn your shoes. Come, we'll be back in time before the kids come out."

Together they head down the hallway hand in hand until reaching an empty room. The aide opens the door and guides Veronica inside before looking down the hallway to see if anyone is coming. The door closes with a "Do Not Disturb, Class in Session" sign swinging back and forth as the curtain closes to block the view inside.

Chapter 16

After picking up Zacori, Veronica decides to take their usual route through Bryant Park. After her encounter in the café, she isn't a patron of their once-favorite shop. Instead, they sit on the bench to talk and reflect on what happened in their day. With Zacori becoming older, Veronica feels he will better understand the truth about his real parents and her future after leaving Keith. If she is going to move on in life and be honest with herself, she feels it is only right to do the same for the child that she loves dearly.

"I have to tell you something today that is very important for you to know," she says.

"What is it?" he asks.

"I'm going to tell you about your parents and I want you to try to understand that they both loved you very much."

"But, I already know that my mom is up in heaven watching over me. You always had me pray to her since I was a kid, right?" Zacori asks.

"That is true. She appointed me to be your mom here when she passed away, and that's why I will always be here for you. It's not that she didn't love you. At the time she just couldn't handle the situation your father was putting her through. Your father is still alive, but…"

"Alive? Alive! My real father is alive? Where?" Zacori asks with excitement. "Is he a traveler somewhere in the safari? Is he coming back soon? Did you speak to him?"

"I wish it was that easy Zacori. When you were very young, your dad did some harsh things and had to go away for quite some time. I used to hear from him when you were younger, but I am sorry to say, it has been years since I have heard anything. He's in jail," Veronica says.

"Jail?"

"I'm sorry, Zacori, but it's true. He has been in prison since you were three years old." Zacori sits on the bench motionless, staring at the ground crying. She takes her hand and rubs it through his shiny blond hair. "It's OK, Zac!" she says.

"I guess no one wanted me but you, huh?"

"That's not true. People go through things in their lives, and sometimes they..."

"I want to see him," Zac says.

"I don't know if that's possible," Veronica stutters, trying to come up with a good answer.

"I want to see him," Zacori demands.

"OK. I will try to locate him and see if we are able to visit him. All I can do is try," says Veronica.

Zacori remains on the bench and begins to swing his feet. He periodically wipes the tears from his face, but never lifts his head. "Can I ask you one more favor?"

"Sure!"

"Do we have to go back home? I don't want to hear all the yelling and fighting anymore. It makes me feel bad that you have to cover your face around people because of what Keith has done. I don't have a lot of money, but I know we can go somewhere for three dollars, right Mom? At least get some potato chips and a juice to share until we find a new home," he says.

Veronica immediately begins to tear up and hug Zacori as tight as she can. "We don't have to go home anymore, sweetheart. From now on it will only be you, and me OK? I will never let anyone hurt us again. I promise," she tells him.

All the stress and pain suddenly disappears from Veronica's body. Her spirit is refreshed. All that is worth living for is sitting right there on the bench next to her. Money has no worth and time has no meaning. The love she needs and was searching for was delivered to her a long time ago. Her vision is blurry from tears as she looks up to the sky and says, "I should have known. I should have known."

∽

Later that evening, she rents a hotel room for a few nights with the money she was able to grab from the closet. Sitting on the edge of the bed while Zacori is sound asleep, Veronica tries to plan out what she will do in the future. Though Keith did not turn out to be the man she thought he was, he is still her husband, and knowing he was with another woman enrages her. It enrages her even more that he has not even made an attempt to contact her or about Zacori's well being at all. Veronica imagines what is going on in her house, and though she is not a fighter, she refuses to be taken for a fool.

"To hell with this," she says, rushing off the bed and double-locking the hotel door behind her to keep Zacori safe. She is going to have her final say, even if it means getting into a fight with Keith.

It takes her around 45 minutes to reach the apartment building. She looks up from the outside to see if there are any lights on, and all was dark. Entering the corridor, she persuades the doorman, who has been working there for years and is someone that she has befriended over time, to let her in with the spare key. He gives her the key without hesitation and she heads upstairs by way of the elevator.

Her stomach quivers with nerves as she watches the numbers slowly light up one by one on the panel until the elevator comes to a sudden halt. She arrives on the apartment floor and peeks her head out first to make sure the coast is clear of any neighbors. She slowly tiptoes down the hallway until reaching the apartment. She places her ear to the door to hear if there is any noise coming from the apartment before slowly entering the key, trying to be as quiet as possible. Poking her head inside, she notices the bedroom door slightly cracked. She enters cautiously, closing the door behind her. With each step closer to the bedroom, her heart beats more and her hands shake with fear.

Soft moans and a squeaking mattress become clearer as she starts tiptoeing towards the back. First she grabs the small lamp that rests on the living room table with one hand, then a knife from the kitchen. Quietly she opens the door, observing Keith making love to another woman in her bed. The mystery is over. As badly as she wants it to be a dream, she is staring at the truth. Gripping her weapons more and more with each thrust Keith delivers, she stands there watching before Fatima looks over Keith's shoulder and notices her. Startled initially, Fatima's eyes open wide in shock, but when she realizes it's Veronica standing there, she begins to smile almost tauntingly. Veronica drops the lamp to the floor. The sound of the lampshade breaking causes Keith to stop, startled as he turns around to see her standing there.

"Why didn't you call before coming here?" he says, fumbling with the sheets to cover himself.

"Why should I call my house when I'm ready to come home? Or should I say *our* house. Would that be more appropriate, Fatima? Our house?"

"We should talk about this. Let me just…"

"Lay your sorry ass down!" Veronica quickly interrupts. "There's no need to talk your about lies anymore, Keith. Not now, not tomorrow, not for the rest of this life we spend on this earth. I don't have to remind you I am your legal wife on paper and I will be taking any amount of money that I deem fit to help me and Zacori survive without any interference while I start over from this hell you put me in. And if you even think about trying to find us to cause us any further harm, I will hunt you down like the dog you are," she says.

Keith angrily begins to pull the sheets off of him to approach Veronica until he sees the blade of the knife shining from her hand. Placing her foot firmly behind her to get leverage, she grips the handle of the knife as firmly as she can. Keith stops on the edge of the bed, cautiously watching Veronica as if he wants to attack.

"You do want to make love again, I assume," Veronica says to Keith, keeping him at bay.

"What are you going to do with that?" he asks laughing, gesturing to the knife.

"Do you really want to find out?" The two look at each other waiting for the next move to be made, but no one budges. Veronica has finally stood up for herself and is ready to put her life on the line to let Keith know she is done. Knowing she has the upper hand, Veronica begins to slowly step back toward the front door, keeping her eyes on Keith the whole time with the knife ready to defend herself. Keith sits on the edge of the bed with Fatima resting her back on the head-rest covered by a blanket. Veronica, still moving backwards, reaches the front door and closes it. She runs to the elevator as fast as she can with her heart racing. Frantically pressing on the button, she waits for the signal that the elevator has arrived, looking down the hall anticipating Keith to come running out after her.

The bell finally signals that the elevator has arrived. She enters quickly, her breaths short and fast. Her heart is racing from the adrenaline. Beads of sweat trickle down the side of her face, and her hands shake nervously. Her eyes begin to fill with pressure as she moves them side-to-side to stay alert. The door begins to close and a sigh of relief begins to fill her body. She stares straight ahead until the wall in front of her begins to narrow. She's startled by the sound of footsteps approaching the elevator and braces herself for the unknown. Suddenly, a hand appears between the doors, causing her to scream as they separate. Terrified, she opens her eyes widely to see who enters. It's the neighbor.

"Hold it!" he yells.

"I thought you were someone else," she says as she gasps for air.

"Are you OK?" he asks.

As the door closes, Veronica looks into the hallway to make sure the coast is clear. "I will be," she responds.

Chapter 17

Ayear has passed and Veronica still remains separated from Keith. Things have not been the greatest financially, but it could always be worse. Keith has never put a stop on his account, giving Veronica the ability to take cash. Even with her thinking about him from time to time and appreciating the fact that he still allows this to happen, she knows in her heart she can never return even if she still loves him. Picking up the pieces and starting all over is never easy for anyone, but Veronica is the rock that can't be broken. Landing a part-time job as a teacher's assistant with the help of the young woman from Zacori's school has given her some hope for a brighter future. She glows and walks with confidence again.

Zacori has also adjusted well to the change. The environment is more peaceful and his grades and overall demeanor are a reflection of it. Every night they still pray together to thank God for blessing them with life and say a few words for Linda. Finally a response has come back from the prison, granting Veronica and Zacori visitation to see Mr. Burns. It is a week away and neither one of them know what to expect, but Zacori really wants to see and speak to his dad. It's something Veronica really doesn't want to do, but he has the right to know who his father is and Mr. Burns deserves to know his son, regardless of his mistakes.

After work she continues their afternoon stroll through the park before going home. Zacori, 12 years old now, has been able to meet a few of the kids whose parents also take the same route. Usually she reads a book or finishes some of the homework the kids hand in, but today is different. Today she actually looks around the park at the people, and sees things for what they truly are. She realizes how many kids are being taken care of by women other than their mothers. There is a massive amount of Caucasian kids being taken care of by minority women. Experience leads her to wonder if most of these kids are the offspring of wealthy parents who don't make time to pick them up from school or take them for walks in the park.

It makes her think. What are these women and men really going through? Is every Asian woman in the park going through the same as Ming? Do other women of color live the same life as hers? How many Lindas are drinking overpriced coffee, praying their husbands never leave? Are all men cheaters and abusers waiting to be exposed? Are all Muslim men bad? Her life experiences have brought about so many questions about reality. All she can do is sit on the bench and remain in a daze as her mind wanders.

During the course of a decade, she has battled with love and religion, family and loss. Her parents have passed on, and her sister has moved on in life. Her sister vowed to never speak to her again after Keith refused to help financially for funeral services and her school. Veronica has lost almost everything in such a short period of time. It seems to her that every time she finds something good, it is followed by a tragedy, but it isn't enough for Veronica to give up. It is her faith alone that keeps her strong enough to get up every day and continue to work hard for her and Zacori.

In Veronica's world there is no shoulder to cry on, no friends or family to run to. At 44 years old, she has accepted that she'll never have children of her own. All she has is Zacori, and that's all she needs. Veronica is at a new beginning. Realizing the world will only look at her as the nanny who cared for a child other than her own and not the friend who never broke her promise, she only wants to get through the next few years peacefully and be able to send Zacori off to college before finally resting and enjoying life.

Every person in the park seems to be in slow motion as she looks on, trying to figure out what could possibly be going on in his or her lives. Sometimes a person's facial expression can tell the whole story of their lives, while others hide behind smiles and laughter to detour others from the truth. In her case, the hijab was the disguise she used to hide the truth, while Linda used money and expensive parties to hide the inner pain she suffered from every day. Veronica begins to understand that every person in some ways has a story to tell. Some live in the fantasy of life, while others face the reality.

Remaining on the bench, her trance is broken up by some form of commotion in the center field. It is hard to ignore the shouts echoing through the park. She decides to walk over in the direction of the kids, remembering Zacori is over there. Once she reaches the outer part of the crowd, she realizes through the dust and bloodthirsty teenagers that it is Zacori fighting. Her first reaction is to immediately break it up, but after seeing he has the upper hand, she lets him go for a few more minutes. After another minute or two, Veronica decides it is enough. She carefully comes between the two, trying to avoid the haymaker blows they are throwing.

"Break it up! Break it up!" she yells as they part. "What is this all about Zacori? I am surprised at your behavior."

Zacori, desperately trying to catch his breath, keeps an eye on his opponent with his fist balled up resting on his knees. "He started it all, Mom! It wasn't my fault," he explains.

"He's a liar! He threw the first punch!" yells the other boy.

"You called my mom a nigger! That's why I hit you!" says Zacori.

Veronica, shocked by what she just heard, tries to keep her composure. "There is no need to put your hands on anyone, even if they say things that could be offensive, so apologize," she says.

Zacori looks to her with confusion and pain in his eyes, but respecting Veronica's wishes, he apologizes. "I'm sorry for hitting you."

"And what else, Zacori?"

He looks at her strangely.

"Apologize for him not being educated enough to know the true definition of words and speaking like a jackass," she says. The crowd begins to laugh at the remarks Veronica's made about the young man. Zacori himself begins to chuckle. "Come on Zacori, we don't have all day. Apologize to the donkey," she reminds him.

"Sorry that you are an uneducated jackass," Zacori says.

"Now let's go," Veronica states, grabbing Zacori around the neck and congratulating him on winning the fight.

"Feels good to win, huh?" she asks.

"Of course!"

An hour later they enter the corridor of the apartment building, where Veronica stops to get the mail from the box. It isn't the best of buildings or the high-priced penthouse some would dream of, but it is home. The keys jingle from her purse as she gives Zacori the OK to go upstairs without her. Grabbing the mail, quickly sorting through it, she notices a letter from the Department of Corrections addressed to her and Zac. *Has Mr. Burns finally answered his son's request to see him, or will it be bad news?* Deciding to read it in the lobby before approaching Zacori, she sits in a squatting position and begins to read:

Dear Veronica:

By the time you receive this letter I pray that your health and happiness continues. I apologize that it has been years since you heard from me last, but in prison sometimes your mind can only allow you to focus on survival. First, I would like to thank you for always being a part of my son's life. I could only imagine the pain and confusion he must be feeling going from house to house all these years with different families. At times

I could have killed myself knowing what I have done to my family, but with an angel on the outside like you, I can sleep a little easier at night. As you very well know, I have done 10 of the 15 years of my sentence and with good behavior and a few programs; it looks as if I may be released in 18 months. Hopefully I can be as successful as before. I definitely know I am smarter. There is so much I can say, but I would rather save my conversation for the day you are able to pick Zacori up and bring him for a visit. I know this isn't the best place for a father to see his son after all these years, but at least it's a start. Visiting days are Monday, Wednesday and Friday from 9-11a.m. then 1-4p.m. You don't have to give advance notice; they will notify me when you arrive. Once again thank you very much for all you have done, and my prayers are with you.

Thank you, Burns.

After reading the letter, Veronica pauses for a moment, confused that Mr. Burns is under the assumption that Zacori was in foster care for all these years. Never did he even know the whereabouts of his son. It saddens her to know that it should not have taken this long for her to get in contact with him and assure him that Zacori was well. In an instance, she takes partial responsibility for depriving a father of his relationship with his son, no matter what the circumstances were. She owes it to Mr. Burns and Zacori to fix the relationship between them. After a few minutes, she goes upstairs to the apartment where Zacori is sitting on the couch already doing his homework. She sits next to him with the letter in her hand.

"I received a letter from your father today," she tells him.

He pauses and places his pen on the notebook. "My real father?" he asks.

"Yes! I was able to write some letters after the discussion we had and locate the prison he is in."

"Did he ask about me? Does he want to see me?"

"He is just as excited about reuniting with you and starting over as you are. To be honest, I felt really bad after reading his letter, because there was no reason the relationship between you two had to stop," she says.

"It's not your fault he made mistakes and ended up in jail," Zacori says, becoming a little irritated.

"Wait a minute, Zacori. A lot of people make mistakes, but it never means that they are bad people. Even though your father made a mistake, nobody has the right to judge him unfairly. The law has already sentenced him, and I am sure he regrets any wrongdoing," she says.

Zacori pauses for a minute before agreeing with Veronica.

"So, I was thinking next week we can take a trip to go and see him," she says.

"Sure, I guess!" Zacori responds, shrugging his shoulders. The room becomes silent as they are obviously in deep thought about what just happened. Veronica fears how Mr. Burns may feel knowing that she was the person who had custody of his son. She is his ex-employee and a friend of his deceased wife. As far as Zacori was concerned, he didn't truly know his father. Mr. Burns was incarcerated since he was three years old, and before that, their relationship wasn't the greatest due to Mr. Burns' work habits. They were still strangers meeting for the first time, no matter who he was biologically. Sensing things are a little awkward; Veronica decides to break the ice.

"Hey! I have a great idea. How about we go see that new Marvel movie you wanted to see, then grab a pizza or something?"

Immediately Zacori's face lights up with cheer. "Really?" he asks with excitement. "What about my homework?"

"You have been doing so well you deserve a treat, and, you did win your first fight today," she says laughing.

"YES!" Zacori yells, jumping from the couch and running toward his room to change.

Excited by all the joy in Zacori's voice, Veronica laughs along with him; knowing only dark days are ahead.

Chapter 18

The Visit

The day has arrived when Zacori will finally have the opportunity to see his father for the first time since he was three years old. It's five o'clock in the morning and he is getting himself together for the long train ride to upstate New York. Veronica can hear him constantly going back and forth from the bed to the bathroom, assuming he is just as nervous as she is, but for different reasons. After the trial Mr. Burns didn't have time to say goodbye to anyone, as he was taken immediately into custody to begin his sentence. There was nothing he could do to control the fate of his son. Yes, he did write letters at the beginning and made periodic phone calls, but now it has become obvious he was under the impression that Zacori's living with Veronica was only temporary until the system decided what was best.

As Veronica prepares some food to take along for the long trip, Zacori sits quietly on the couch tossing his basketball in the air. *I wonder what's going on his mind*, she thinks to herself while glancing over to him.

"Are you OK?" she asks.

"I guess so," he answers.

Knowing something is wrong, Veronica stops what she is doing for the moment and takes a seat next to him on the couch for support.

"Nervous, huh?" she asks. He sits there quietly as though he didn't hear the question. She places her arms around his shoulder while giving him a slight kiss on the side of his head. "It'll be OK, Zacori."

"What if he sees me and still doesn't want me?" he asks.

"That's not going to happen. Your father will take one look at you and be just as happy to see you as anyone in the world. Who knows, he may be just as nervous right now as you are. I bet he's thinking, what if you don't want him," she says.

"Will you be there with me the whole time?"

"If you want me to. Of course, I have to give you guys time to talk, bond, asks questions, and get to know each other as much as possible for the short time that you will have with one another today. But I will definitely not leave you." The clock reads 6:30 and Veronica realizes she has to get herself together. "Have I ever left you before?" she asks, trying to get him to laugh, rubbing her knuckles into his dirty blond hair.

"No, but they did," he says.

"Remember what I always told you. You can't live your life holding onto the past or trying to make sense of things that are out of your control. Sometimes God puts people in your life that may not be the best, but it's his way to have you learn a lesson and become a better person. So don't live life with a sour heart, but an open mind. OK?"

"OK," he says.

"So on that note young man, you can help me finish getting the lunches together, because we have a four-hour train ride ahead of us."

Zacori quickly embraces Veronica with a firm hug, resting his head in her chest. "Thanks, Mom," he mumbles.

"Everything will be OK, as long as you believe it will," she says looking towards the sky.

Once she reaches the train station, Veronica looks carefully for the departure times of trains stopping at Dannemora Hills, where Clinton Correctional Facility is located. With a little time to spare before the train departs, they take a seat, placing the bags on the ground in the waiting area. Glancing around at some of the passengers, she notices a lot of the women have children with them and some are by themselves.

Analyzing the women, Veronica can only assume they're visiting the prison also. Many are breathtakingly beautiful. A few are obviously students, reading textbooks or doing schoolwork on laptops. These women are highly motivated to become educated or at least on their way. It dawns on her that a lot of these women are keeping the family together by themselves while their husbands or children's fathers are incarcerated. There is a woman of every race, shape and form there, from upper-class women like Linda to regular 9-to-5 working women struggling to just make it in life. There are a lot of guys there also, some you wouldn't want to see in an alley late at night. Whatever the reason, they are there for the incarcerated. *Is it loyalty or love?* She thinks to herself.

A horn blows, followed by an announcement. "Now boarding on track six to Dannemora Hills. All aboard!" the conductor yells.

Quickly the waiting area comes to life with everyone gathering their belongings and children to not miss the train. Veronica taps Zacori on the leg, gesturing to him that it's time to go. She hands the conductor their tickets before boarding the train looking for their assigned seats. Zacori races to get the window, and Veronica sits close to the aisle. Almost instantly, she can't help but to notice the young fair-skinned lady sitting next to her with a blanket covering her chest like a scroll. Tiny toes stick out from the blanket, wiggling in the air. Obviously the young woman is breastfeeding. It comes as a shock to her because all the young women she meets use bottles or formula. Breastfeeding is something commonly seen at home in Africa, and it touches Veronica to see a woman giving some of herself to keep the child healthy.

There is no denying that Veronica has many regrets about not being able to have children of her own, but it is out of her hands. It's God's decision, she thinks.

Looking up and smiling, the young woman adjusts the blanket to make sure her breasts aren't exposed. "Excuse me!" she says.

"No, I'm sorry. Excuse me for staring. It's just that I haven't seen many women breastfeeding here, and it just took me to some memories of my country when I saw you," Veronica says.

"No, it's fine."

Veronica gets settled in her seat when Zacori asks how long the ride is.

"I think it's anywhere from five to six hours. I am not truly sure," she responds.

"It's four and a half hours," says the young woman with her head now on the headrest. "Four and a half long hours!"

"I assume this isn't your first trip?" says Veronica.

"I have been making this trip for the last eight months. After the economy had a meltdown, I had to travel out of the city just to find work. My husband does the best he can working at night, but it's still not enough. So, every other day I have to take this trip upstate to clean the houses of some families I know. It doesn't pay much, but it helps with the bills. Plus, they pay for my travel and my kids get to see something different from the concrete jungle of the city. And you?"

"Well! I'm going to the…"

"I know. You're going to the prison. I have been taking this trip long enough to know most of the faces and where the majority of the passengers are going. It's nothing to be embarrassed about. It doesn't mean they're bad people." She laughs. "Hey, look at me. I have a husband at home to help me and together we're still poor. I would love to have formula or afford milk, but I was denied public assistance before we had two incomes. We barely cover rent, so to feed my child I expose my breasts on the train to keep him healthy. What a life, huh?" She begins to rub the cover where the child's head would be. "But it's all worth it at the end of the day."

Veronica simply shakes her head in agreement; understanding the sacrifice the woman is going through. She wraps her arms around Zacori as the train begins to pull off. "Here we go, Zacori," she tells him as he stares out of the window.

Tired from getting up early, Veronica decides to close her eyes and catch up on some sleep before the train arrives at the prison. A loud horn echoes throughout the cart, awakening Veronica. She looks over to Zacori, who remains cuddled up in his chair. Placing her jacket over him for warmth, she glances over to the young woman, who isn't awakened by the horn. Still a little disoriented, Veronica stretches and then realizes that the baby is being held by a male figure looking out the window. She can't see his face, but is not alarmed because the baby is quiet. She pulls a book from her bag, trying not to pay attention or impose on anyone around her.

For some reason, Veronica can't help but to glance in the direction of the gentleman sitting quietly looking out the window. He sits with perfect posture, fondling religious beads between his fingers. As Veronica's nerves and anxiety grow, her hairs stand up. She can hear the air coming through her lips as she glances at the beads from the corner of her eyes, one by one moving between his fingers. She clears her throat, repositioning herself in an attempt to relax before hearing a familiar voice.

"Did you really think I would never find you?" it says.

Her eyes widen as her heart rate increases to an alarming beat. Unable to move, she sits paralyzed in her chair, refusing to look in any direction but straight.

"Did you hear me?" the voice asks.

"What do you want from us?"

He turns to face her. Her biggest fear has come true. Keith is the voice she feared. By the time Veronica looks over, the young lady and Keith are staring in her direction.

"Did you truly believe I would allow you to just walk out on me and continue using my money to feed and educate a child that isn't mine? I always thought you were smarter than that," he says.

He passes the baby over to the young woman, who only puts her head down after receiving the child. Keith begins to stand

and climb over the woman as Veronica frantically shakes Zacori awake. It seems as if time is moving in slow motion. Keeping her eyes on Keith the whole time, she screams desperately to wake Zacori up.

"Help! Help!" she cries. "Zacori, please wake up!"

Slowly Zacori begins to open his eyes. "Mom! Mom!" he says tugging on her arm.

Keith has now made his way over and lifts his hand to strike her. Raising her arms to shield herself from the blow, she can see the rage in his eyes before she braces for the blow. All she can hear is Zacori's voice calling her as she stares into the darkness.

"Mom, wake up! It's our stop. Come on, let's go," he says.

Her eyes open to see the sunlight shining brightly on her face from the window with Zacori tugging on her sleeve. Still startled, Veronica looks around, only to realize that she was having a bad dream. Gathering her belongings, she glances at the young woman, who remains sleeping with her baby resting. Knowing firsthand how hard times can be, Veronica reaches into her purse and pulls out most of the money brought on the trip, placing it on the chair. She begins to walk out of the car before turning around and saying, "God bless you, sister," before joining Zacori on the platform.

Veronica follows the instructions on the signs posted that inform passengers where to proceed if they are taking a bus to the prison. Boarding for a 20-minute ride that will finally end what has become an exhausting trip, they ride along the countryside of upstate New York fascinated by the beauty nature has to offer. Accustomed to the dreaded scenery of the concrete jungle, it feels good to see trees, lakes and farmland that many people forget about living in the inner city. This small town is reminiscent of a time when people still cared for one another. Signs are posted along the highway for upcoming events that will be hosted by the local high schools. Families support local farmers by purchasing produce from acres of fields.

"Five minutes!" yells the driver.

They continue up a small dirt road surrounded by acres of open grass where men in orange jumpsuits work while being watched by corrections officers with rifles. A large, dark gray castle sits alone in the middle of nowhere, with small annexed buildings surrounding it. It is cold and emotionless, with large barbed wire coiled along the walls. Two officers looking through binoculars with rifles resting on their backs guard the watchtower.

Arriving at the front, they stand outside a large steel fence in a perfect line before a buzzing sound signal the unlocking of the outside gate. Once inside, they are met by guards who continue assisting them, only here dogs accompany them. Many women are escorted off the line immediately for inappropriate clothing and told to either change or come back another day. The group is split into two groups, men to the left and women to the right.

"Please remove all items from your pockets. Cell phones and other mechanical devices off from this point on. Upon reaching the metal detectors, shoes must be off, along with any hats and belts," an officer shouts.

Veronica approaches one of the officers who stands firmly with his arms folded, observing the crowd. He is a fairly large, well-built gentleman with a scar on the side of his face that goes from his ear to the lower part of his cheek. His shirt is white, differentiating him from the others. He seems experienced, his eyes moving side-to-side taking a mental photograph of each person entering.

"Excuse me, sir," Veronica says to get his attention. He simply moves his head, acknowledging her. "I have never been here before. My son is only 13. I was just wondering if he could…" She is suddenly interrupted by his deep voice.

"Does he piss standing up, ma'am?"

"Well, of course," she says, trying to find humor in his response.

"Then he goes with the men to be searched on their line, and it's not negotiable." He points. Over there, or your visit is denied."

If Veronica doesn't understand anything else, it is clear that in prison, even as a visitor the rules are to be followed. She assures

Zacori that everything will be fine and he has to go on the line with the men until search process is over. She stands on a line slowly moving forward as each lady enters a dimly lit room. In the distance, she can see female officers with rubber gloves moving back and forth calling out "NEXT" every few minutes. It's her turn to enter the room. To the right, women and young children gather their things, barely dressed and in a rush. The walls are a dirty grayish blue with fluorescent lights shining in the area where visitors stand.

"All right ladies! We need all articles of clothing removed down to the underwear. Place your clothing on the table and put your arms up. If you have any contraband, let us know now, because if we find it, your visit will become permanent. Let's go! Hurry up," a female officer yells.

Some of the women are so accustomed to the rules that they've already undressed before the officer finishes speaking. Others know some of the COs on a first-name basis. *If the women are treated as inmates, how are the men when they visit?* She thinks to herself. She worries about how Zacori is feeling, knowing it is probably scary for a child this young. After the search is done, she proceeds down a corridor where Zacori is already waiting, leaning against the bars.

"Are you OK, honey? Those guys can be pretty scary, huh?" she asks.

"It wasn't too bad. They asked me whom I was here to see, I walked through the metal detectors really quickly, and before I knew it, I was told to wait here until you came out," he says.

"Really?" Veronica asks, shocked at what she's hearing.

"Yeah, Mom. Everybody knows most of the contraband that comes in jail is either from visiting women or officers," Zacori says with confidence.

"And how would you know that?"

"They talk about it all the time on the TV show 'Locked Up.'"

"I need to pay more attention to what you watch, young man. Are you ready?"

"Sure!"

They enter a small cafeteria, where an officer stands with a clipboard telling the visitors where to sit before the arrival of the inmates. "Burns," Veronica says.

"Burns. You will be sitting at table 15. Just give us a few minutes and he'll be right down. Have a good day."

"Thank you! Let's go, Zac."

Walking through the room they feel as if all eyes are on them. She rubs Zacori's shoulder, noticing that inmates are strategically seated so they will have no eye contact with each other.

They finally reach the table and sit. "We're here, table 15," Veronica says.

After 10 minutes the wait is finally over. Mr. Burns arrives behind the steel bars and is searched one final time before entering. Zacori isn't able to recognize him after all these years, but Veronica knows immediately it is him. He still stands erect, with his gray hair combed back and beige khakis sharply pressed. After all these years he still looks the same, as if jail has postponed his aging process. He looks around to see if he recognizes anyone. Veronica puts her hand up to signal their location. He looks over himself to make sure he's neat and uses his hand to go over his hair, and then approaches the table. Veronica taps Zacori on the shoulder to get his attention before nodding her head toward his dad. Once Mr. Burns sits at the table, they make eye contact immediately.

Mr. Burns reaches his hand out. "Hello Zac."

Zacori continues to sit in his chair with his hands resting on his lap. Realizing how hard this may be for Zacori, especially with Keith being the only male figure in his life up until this point, Veronica reaches out to Mr. Burns. "He must be a little shy right now. It's so good to see you, Mr. Burns," she says, extending her hand to his.

"It's truly good to see you too, Veronica. Who would have ever thought after all this time you would be the one to reconnect me and my son. I truly want to thank you for all you have done. I mean every word of it," he says.

"It's fine. Zac has truly been a blessing," she says, looking over to Zacori, whose head is down.

"Zacori, say hello to your father."

"HE'S NOT MY FATHER!" Zacori shouts. "I'm ready to go!"

Veronica, embarrassed, attempts to smile.

"It's OK, Zac. I understand how you may feel. I would feel the same way if I were in your shoes. If you can give me a few minutes to just explain to you my mistakes, it may help things," Mr. Burns says.

"I am going over there so you guys can have some son and father time," Veronica says.

Before she stands, Zacori grabs her hand. "Mom, don't go too far OK?"

"Sure, Zac. I will be right over there by the wall."

Mr. Burns curiously looks at Zacori and then at Veronica after he calls her mom. He remains silent until Veronica walks off. She stands by the main doorway observing the two of them talk. About 20 minutes have gone by and it seems they may have gained some ground. Periodically she sees them smiling and Mr. Burns touching Zacori's head. It makes her feel good that she was able to get them back together. As much as she loves Zacori, the fact remains she isn't his biological mother.

Meanwhile at the table, the conversation seems to be going pretty well between Mr. Burns and Zacori. Zacori turns in his chair to see where Veronica is, making brief eye contact before he turns back around.

"I am so happy you came to see me today," says Mr. Burns.

"It was Mom who really searched for you after she told me that you were still around, or existed for that matter," Zacori responds.

Mr. Burns pauses for a moment. "Let me ask you, Zacori. Do you understand that Veronica is not your real mom?"

"I know my real mom killed herself, but that doesn't matter to me. The only thing that matters to me is that she is the only mother I had a chance to love, and I know she loved me," Zacori firmly states.

"You're right. You're absolutely correct, and I don't mean to offend you or her. All I can wish for is that you let me have the chance to be a dad. I know this is not the way to raise a child, but I will be out of here soon, and I would love to make up for lost time. What do you say, buddy?" Mr. Burns asks, extending his hand to Zacori to signal an agreement. "I promise to be the best dad when this is over."

Zacori hesitates for a minute before shaking Mr. Burns' hand. Mr. Burns stands up. "Is it OK if I have a hug?" Mr. Burns asks.

Zacori stands and gives his father a hug. A voice yells "No physical contact, Burns. Sit down."

"Come on, it's my son. I almost forgot I was in jail for a moment," Mr. Burns says.

Veronica begins to make her way back over to the table where the two of them are laughing. "Please, Veronica, have a seat," Mr. Burns suggests. "Zac has told me all the wonderful things you have done for him over the years. I just wanted to tell you in front of him that I truly appreciate it. All this time, I thought he was in foster care or adopted. It gives me a good feeling to know it was you who cared for him all these years, and I promise to try to be a better father when my time is over here. Isn't that right buddy?"

"Sure!" Zacori answers.

"Well, that's all I ever really wanted for him. Once he was old enough to understand, I had to find you. I know how much he always wanted a father," she says, looking at Zacori.

"You mean to tell me you put your whole life on hold for Zac?" Mr. Burns asks.

"Well I was married, but it didn't work out like I planned. You remember Keith from the Christmas party many moons ago?" she asks.

Mr. Burns pauses to think. "Yes, I do, really nice guy. Very clean and respectful. Damn! That's the last one I had before, well you know. Look, our time is almost done and I would really appreciate if Zacori can attend more visits. Can I have a number to reach you so I can call from time to time? If that's OK, of course."

"What'll you say, Zac?" Veronica asks.

"Um, OK." Zac answers.

"Great! You can leave it with the front, and they'll give it to me. As you can see, they're pretty strict on touching. You should see their rules on sharp objects – not very popular around here obviously," Mr. Burns chuckles.

"No problem. Zac, are you ready to go?" she asks.

"Yeah. Talk to you later, Dad," Zacori says.

"Definitely, son. Definitely," Mr. Burns responds.

As they walk off, Mr. Burns remains at the table to watch them exit. A Caucasian guard approaches the table to take him back to his cell. "Who was that, rich boy?" he jokingly asks.

Mr. Burns stands, smirking. "Just the nigger who kidnapped my kid."

Chapter 19

The phone rings. Veronica rests on the couch reading the newspaper, as she does every Sunday morning. She identifies the number on the caller ID as the correctional facility where Mr. Burns is. Ever since the initial visit, Mr. Burns has called every Sunday to speak with Zacori. Today Zacori isn't home, but she decides to answer and have a conversation with Mr. Burns.

"Yes, I agree to the call." It takes a few seconds before Mr. Burns actually speaks.

"Hey Veronica, how are you? I called to speak to Zacori. Is he there?"

"I'm well, Mr. Burns. Zacori is usually here at this time knowing that you call, but today he's late. Knowing him, he probably stayed a little longer at the park where all the kids skateboard."

"Wow, he didn't tell me that he was a skater."

"He's not just a skater; he is one of the best. I actually saw him a few weeks ago and he was awesome. The crowd just shouted his name and applauded him, and it was great," Veronica says.

"It's those little things that I miss the most," Mr. Burns states as he chokes with emotion. I wasted so much time working and doing other things that I lost focus on my family. If being incarcerated hasn't taught me anything else, it's that nothing is more important than family."

"That's true! I don't know what I would have done all the years without Zacori in my life. He is the only family I have," she responds.

They pause from the conversation for a moment, each reflecting on their comments about family. Veronica simply listens as Mr. Burns weeps before getting himself together. "I wanted to talk to you about that. As you know, Zac is the only family I have left in my life also, and I was just informed that I would be released a little earlier than I thought for good behavior. I appreciate all you have done, truly I have, but when I get out and get on my feet I think Zacori needs to be with the only parent he has left. He needs to know who he is and where he came from, you know."

Veronica holds the phone in her hand, just staring at it. She understands exactly what he means, and it is to take the only person in her life that means something to her. "Hello? Are you still there? Hello?" Mr. Burns repeats.

"How dare you?" Veronica asks before slamming the phone onto the receiver with anger.

Later that afternoon once Zacori returns home, Veronica decides to have a discussion with him about her conversation with his father. She knew that one day after all these years she would have to face the fact that Mr. Burns might come for him, but before any decision is made Zacori deserves an explanation. They sit to have lunch. Veronica knows that as long as he is eating, he will be listening.

"Your dad called today while you were out skateboarding," she says.

"Aw, man! It's Sunday. How could I have been so stupid? I knew he was going to call. What did he say? Is he going to call back?"

"I am not sure, to be honest with you. I mean, of course he will call back, but I don't know if it will be today."

"OK, I'll apologize when he calls," Zacori responds.

"He and I spoke briefly about something today, and I wanted to hear your opinion on it."

"Sure! What was it?"

"Well, your dad will be released a little earlier than he intended, and…he asked…well…basically…"

She tries to finish but is interrupted by Zacori jumping out of his chair with excitement, shouting yes. "That's great. When is he coming out? My dad is coming out!" he shouts.

As much as it hurts Veronica to know Mr. Burns' wishes, she can't interrupt the joy in Zacori's face. She sits in the chair smiling, watching him enjoy the moment.

"Did he say when?"

"Not really. I know it may be soon by the way he sounded. He's just as excited as you and can't wait to pick up the pieces and be the dad you always wanted," she tells him.

"That's awesome! We owe all it all to you, Mom. Thanks," he says, wrapping his arms around her neck.

"There's nothing I wouldn't do for you," she says, hugging Zacori just as tight. "Oh, there's one more thing before I forget. I'm still the boss. Don't forget, tonight is your night for dishes. Hurry up and eat so you can bust the suds, sir," she jokes.

"I know. It sure will be good having my dad around. There's so much we are going to do together," he says.

"Well I'm sure the two of you will make the best of the time that you spend together," Veronica responds.

Zacori rushes eating his food. Veronica sits quietly in the chair observing him eat, knowing in the back of her mind that bad days are approaching. Her face shows a smile, but her soul is crying inside.

"Don't choke trying to eat faster than you can chew, Zacori."

"I just don't want to miss the phone if my Dad calls back. Are we still going to see him in two weeks?" he asks.

"Of course. I will get the train tickets tomorrow. I am glad you reminded me; I almost forgot with all the school work I have to go over," she says.

"You should bring it with you when we visit. While Dad and I are talking it'll give you something to do," Zacori says, unaware that his comment has deeply hurt Veronica. She realizes that it will only be a matter of time before he will forget all about her and want to be with his dad. He is a young man who needs male guidance and companionship. If his father is willing to step back in his life and Zacori accepts it, she will allow it as long as he is treated correctly. She wonders what Linda would say about this if she were still living. She can't imagine what life would be without Zac. What would she do? Who would she care for, and who would care for her?

The phone rings. Veronica looks up at the clock to check the time and hears Zacori's footsteps rapidly moving throughout the apartment to answer the phone. She makes sure to position herself so she can overhear his conversation.

"Yes, I'll accept. Hey, Dad. What? Are you kidding me? Two weeks – that's awesome! Veronica told me something about that when I got home." Slowly she stands and begins walking toward her bedroom sorrowfully before closing the door. All she can do is sit on the edge of the bed and wipe the tears from her face after hearing Zacori call her by her name. Her heart is broken and her spirit shattered. The more she thinks of what may come, the more nauseated she becomes. Deep down, she knows it's only a matter of time before she once again loses someone.

Chapter 20

Life After Zacori

It's been two weeks since Zacori's father announced he would be released. They never made the trip to see him as planned. Deep down she didn't want to, and as selfish as it seemed, Veronica felt she could save her money to do something else. Even without the visit, Zacori has spoken to his father on Sundays as they always have. She can't deny him that.

This is the week of Mr. Burns' release. Of course he knows where she lives, so to avoid seeing him she leaves the house early every day. He doesn't know where she works, so at least she has time before they will see each other. Veronica wakes up early, and Zacori is already up and ready. To her surprise, he's even prepared her lunch today.

"Are we up and ready for school today, young man?" She asks.

"I couldn't sleep last night. My dad told me he would be released yesterday or today. I just have so many plans for us later," he replies.

"You didn't tell me your father might have been released yesterday. I think that would have been something important for me to know. In case he wanted to come over, at least the house would have been clean," she says nervously, attempting to laugh. Veronica rubs her hands vigorously as her nerves build up.

"I would have, but he told me not to tell you. He wanted to do something special for you, for all you have done over the years, so I promised to keep it a secret."

"Really? That's cool I guess," she says. "I would have thought the complete opposite, but OK."

"I was thinking maybe I could escort you to work today. It's not that far from my school, so do you think it'll be OK?"

"What are you up to, young man? You have that look in your eye. We have to leave now for you to be on time."

Quickly gathering the things they need for the day, the two of them head out the door to get on the train. As Zacori enters the hallway, Veronica locked the door. "Did your Dad say what the surprise was?"

"No. Can we just hurry please?" he says in a rush, giggling devilishly.

An hour later they exit the train station laughing and joking, headed toward the school. Veronica sets her arm on Zacori's shoulder, smiling with every step, enjoying the time they are spending together.

"You know, I'm glad you decided to escort me to work this morning. It feels like I have a young handsome chaperone," she says.

"My pleasure, Mom," he responds.

The closer they get, the more visible the police cars parked in front of the school become. At first Veronica thinks maybe one of the kids pulled the fire alarm or started fighting early until she sees a familiar face. Mr. Burns and a teacher's assistant are talking to an officer who is taking notes while they speak. It seems they are definitely in a confrontation.

"Hey, is that my dad?" Zacori asks.

"I think so, but what is he doing up here, and why? Zacori, did you tell your father where I work?"

He hesitates for a moment. "Yes, but only because he said he wanted to surprise you with something special. What is going on, Mom?"

"I don't know, but I think we need to find out," she says, approaching the front of the school.

Once they come in contact with everyone, she realizes her friend has her hands over her mouth with tears coming down her face, while Mr. Burns points in Veronica's direction. Two officers begin to walk toward her and everything becomes silent. Her hand drops off Zacori's shoulder trembling because she knows whatever is about to happen is not good as the officers approach her with caution.

"Are you Veronica Owuso?" one asks.

Hesitant and scared, she replies yes. The other officer stands next to Zacori before asking his name. "What going on, officers?" Veronica asks.

"Ma'am, we'll inform you once the young man answers the question." Zacori looks up to Veronica, unsure of what to do or say.

"It's OK, Zacori, answer the officer."

"Yes, I'm Zacori Burns."

"Do you identify the man across the street as your father?"

"Yes, he's my father. What did he do?" he asks, all the while looking at Mr. Burns.

"He didn't do anything. Can you step across the street where your father is please? Ma'am we're going to ask that you wait here for a moment, please, just for precaution."

Zacori makes his way across the street to his waiting dad, who greets him with a hug looking concerned. Meanwhile, the officer begins to question Veronica.

"Ma'am my name is Detective Lewis and I just want to ask you a few questions."

"Sure!" Veronica says, watching Mr. Burns and Zacori as they both look on. She notices that her friend remains crying and shaking her head while observing the interaction between Veronica and the officers.

"My first question is, who has the rightful custody of Zacori Burns?"

"When his mother died, she asked me to take responsibility for him until he was able to be on his own."

"Did you ever notify the courts or his biological father of his mother's request?"

"No, but his father went to jail. What's this all about, officer?" she asks.

154

"Ma'am can you please place your hands behind your back?"

Veronica becomes hysterical. "Why? What's going on here? What are you doing?" She screams as the detective grabs her arm, forcing her hand behind her. "What did I do? What did I do?"

"Veronica Owuso, you are under arrest for the kidnapping of Zacori Burns."

As the officer informs her of her rights, she screams, "No! Please, somebody help me. Mr. Burns how can you do this to me? Please don't do this to me. I did nothing wrong. I raised him. Please, Mr. Burns!"

Zacori, seeing what's happening, tries to run over as Mr. Burns grabs him. "No Zacori, it's for the best," he says before Zacori manages to wiggle himself free.

"What are you doing?" yells Zacori as he runs across the street and begins a shoving match with one of the officers, trying to get to Veronica. As people watch, the two of them desperately reach for each other before Veronica is placed in the police car and Zacori drops to his knees, screaming, "Sorry, Mom! I am so sorry." He watches his mother being driven away in a squad car, desperately looking at him like a puppy in a cage until she fades away in the distance. Still on his knees in the middle of the street, Zacori is completely distraught by what his father has tricked him into.

Mr. Burns approaches and kneels down next to him. "Son, I know how you may feel, but I promise you that..." Zacori turns and spits in his face, jumping on his back. "Zac wait! I am your father," Mr. Burns says as Zacori continues to take shots at him.

"YOU'RE NOT MY FATHER!" he says.

An officer on the scene suddenly separates the two and Zacori is escorted away by a woman. The officer restrains Mr. Burns as he yells, "I did it for us! Don't you understand? We are family. She is not your mother. You were brainwashed and kidnapped by a stranger. You have to believe me!"

﹌

Later that day, Veronica is in a room at the precinct waiting for someone to enter and thinking about what Mr. Burns is up to. *God! I can't even make a phone call. Who am I going to call? I can't afford a lawyer nor do I even know one, for that matter,* she thinks to herself.

The door opens and Detective Lewis and another gentleman enter the room with cups of hot coffee, placing them on the table. "Would you like some sugar or cream before we start?" Detective Lewis asks. Veronica agrees to sugar. "Do you know what's going on here, Veronica? Is it OK for me to call you Veronica?"

"No, I don't know what's going on, and Veronica is fine."

"I see," the detective responds before pouring two sugars in her coffee. "Let me explain. Three days before Mr. Burns' release, he called us stating that he was able to find his son after all his years of being incarcerated. Now, according to Mr. Burns, you took his child at a very trying time in his parents' lives and took it upon yourself to raise him. Are any of these things true?"

"No! I never would have taken care of Zacori all these years if his own mother did not ask me to before her suicide. I was the one who reached out to find where Mr. Burns was being held. He never tried to find his son," says Veronica.

"Why didn't you come to the authorities or family court and let his mother's wishes be known or that you had him? You have to admit, this story does seem a little unrealistic, don't you think?"

"It may sound crazy, but every word I say is true. When his mother committed suicide in my apartment, my fiancé and I read the letter in which she asked me to keep him safe. I swear to you – you can locate my ex-husband and ask him," she desperately pleads.

"Your ex, huh? That wouldn't be Hasim Ahmed, a.k.a Keith, would it?"

"Yes, it would be. He will tell you everything," she says.

"We already spoke with him, and he has no recollection of ever being with you. And, by the way, let's just say he has his hands full with 'affairs' in the mosque, so I doubt he'll be participating

156

in this case. Here's a question. How did you manage to send him to school and doctors all these years?"

Veronica takes a sip of the coffee and remains quiet. A single tear rolls down her face as her hands shake with nervousness. She knows she is in serious trouble and that it will take a miracle to get out of it. The detective keeps talking but his words are lost in Veronica's head. *After all these years and sacrifices, this is how it's going to end*, she thinks to herself. As she reflects on her life, she remembers Linda's face, the decor of the mosque, brutal beatings from Keith, good times shared with Zacori, and the last images of her parents. The detective asking her a question suddenly interrupts her.

"Do you want to talk to a lawyer? Do you wish to seek counsel?"

"Yes, please," she answers.

"You will be held until counsel arrives to speak with you."

The detective shakes his head as they exit the room. Veronica remains in the chair and slowly sips on the coffee. Meanwhile, behind the glass, a room of people witnesses the questioning. One person all too familiar with Mr. Burns and his past is the district attorney, who put him away 13 years ago and remembers Veronica from court.

"I remember this woman," she says.

"From where?" a gentleman asks.

"She was the friend of the wife in Mr. Burns' case. His wife committed suicide in her apartment, I believe," she says.

"So what do we do? Open the door and set her free? That's not going to happen," says the gentleman.

"I understand that, but we are not going to just let her be bait for a room of sharks. I need the best on this case to represent her. I can almost guarantee she will plead not guilty, because she isn't. I want you to call Amy on this one," she says.

"No disrespect, but this is a clear case of a woman who took the law in her own hands and I believe..."

"And I believe I'm the district attorney still, so I need Amy on this one. Are my orders clear or do we still have a misunderstanding?"

She firmly says to the gentleman, who simply puts his hands up in agreement and takes his cell phone out to begin dialing. The D.A. folds her arms and stares into the glass. Sensing someone is behind the glass watching her, Veronica turns to the glass and stares at it.

The gentleman informs the D.A. the call has been made. "Amy will be in your office in 20 minutes."

"Good. Now she has a lawyer." The district attorney continues staring into the glass, feeling a connection to Veronica on the other side.

Chapter 21

Now that Veronica has been arrested, Zacori's future remains unknown. Mr. Burns sits in the waiting area of the ACS building waiting to speak with the newly appointed social worker now involved in Zacori's case. He thinks if Veronica is out of the way, Zacori will automatically be turned over to his custody.

"Mr. Burns, you can come in now," says the social worker.

Mr. Burns stands to enter her office. She signals for him to sit before opening the folder to review the case. "OK, Mr. Burns. I see that you're indeed Zacori's father by the paperwork you've produced for us. I think the first thing we must go over is the procedure…"

"What procedure? He's my son and I want him with me," he says arrogantly. I'm no longer incarcerated, so what's the problem?"

"The first problem is your tone. The second problem is that this child hasn't been in your presence for years while you were incarcerated. Needless to say, you're also on parole."

"And that means what to me?"

"Who cares what it means to you? To the state of New York, it means your residence must be checked and you must show us a stable source of income before your court date."

"Court date? Why do I have to go to court to see my son? I am a very rich man still, my dear, and there is no doubt I can give my son more than that black – excuse me, kidnapper could ever have."

"Maybe, but that will have to be proven. Remember something sir – it really doesn't matter how you may feel or what I personally think about the woman accused of taking your son. My job is to put him in a stable environment with the person or people who can do the best for him. For now he will be placed in one of our state residences, where food and shelter will be provided for him until a judge determines what's next."

Mr. Burns sits in his chair with his face red as a tomato, furious at what the social worker has just told him. "So you mean to tell me my son will be placed in a home instead of a comfortable bed with his father?"

"You should have thought about that 13 years ago sir. Have a good day. We will be in touch," she says, smirking at him.

"Bullshit!" he says before standing and exiting her office.

"Don't forget to leave your contact information, sir!" she yells from her desk.

9 a.m. Veronica has spent her first night in jail thinking about what she can do to get out of this. She is scheduled to see the judge later, and has no idea what she could say to make him or her believe that her intentions were good, that she only did it for Zacori and the promise made to Linda.

If I would only have kept that letter, she thinks.

"Veronica?" asks the guard standing in front of the cell.

"Yes, that's me," she responds.

"Let's go. Your attorney is here to speak to you. Gather your things; your time is limited."

Quickly grabbing her jacket, she exits the cell to see who her attorney is. She arrives upstairs to where the attorney is waiting and two Caucasian women looking through notepads are talking. Together they stand, realizing Veronica has entered into the room. The guard takes off the handcuffs and points to where Veronica should sit. Each of the attorneys extends their hand to formally introduce themselves to her.

"Hello, Veronica. I'm Amy Lawson, and this is Jennifer Horowitz. We'll be your attorneys for this case. Please sit."

"I have to let you know that I don't know how I will be able to pay you for your service. I'm barely able to make it day to day," Veronica says.

The attorneys look at each other and smile. "We are not here to get paid. We represent women from many countries – missionaries, nonprofit health organization workers and regular women like yourself," says Jennifer.

"Wow! How did you hear of me?" Veronica asks.

"Let's just say somebody from the past remembered and appreciated something you did. We need to know everything about the last 13 years up until you were arrested. Take your time. The more we know, the better we can help you," Amy states.

Veronica takes a deep breath as Jennifer presses record on the small recorder placed on the table. "Well, it all started at a small coffee shop where I first met Linda and her son Zacori years ago..."

3 p.m. Veronica waits handcuffed inside a small area in the back of the courthouse designated for inmates waiting to see the judge. Quietly she avoids conversation with any of the other ladies. She can hear some of the women who are obviously experienced in the system telling others what to say and what they can expect in court. It can almost be considered a heads-up session because a lot of the information is very useful, but after meeting Amy and Jennifer this morning, Veronica knows she is in good hands.

A female officer approaches the doorway. "Veronica Owuso." She looks up and nods her head. With each step she takes toward the courtroom, the lights get brighter. As she enters the courtroom, Amy and Jennifer stand erect behind a desk with a tall Caucasian man adjacent to them at another. The judge, an older Caucasian gentleman with streaks of gray, sits up high in the bench writing as the court officers escort Veronica to her chair. Amy and Jennifer's faces show they mean business.

"Your Honor, this is case #27348: The State of New York vs. Veronica Owuso," says the officer.

The judge takes the document and proceeds to look through it. "Do we have counsel representing the defendant?" he asks.

"Yes, Your Honor."

The judge looks up and makes a face. "I see. Hello counselor. Nice to see you in my courtroom again," he sarcastically remarks.

"Pleasure, your Honor."

"So let's see what we have here! Kidnapping and endangering the welfare of a child," says the judge. "How do you plead?"

"My client pleads not guilty. The child was held strictly on the wishes of his deceased mother while his father was serving a 15-year sentence, Your Honor," Jennifer says.

"Your honor, whether the act was of good faith or not, the authorities were never properly notified of the child's whereabouts to determine what was best. Also, the child was three at the time. How do we know what the deceased mother's wishes were? Even though the father was incarcerated, he still had legal paternal rights over his son. He was never notified by Ms. Owuso of his son's whereabouts until the child was old enough to ask about him and sought to find him," says the prosecutor.

"Mr. Burns was fully aware of his son's whereabouts upon entering into the correctional system. We will prove his negligence as a father is what made our client become the primary caretaker of his son," Jennifer says.

"Am I correct to assume we will be moving toward a pre-trial hearing, unless there has been a plea bargain agreement?" asks the judge.

"That is correct, Your Honor," Amy says.

"Has a bail agreement been discussed?" the judge asks.

"The state asks that bail be denied after discovering the defendant may be a flight risk. We have learned that her native country is Ghana and she is not a legal citizen of this country at this time. The state would like to keep tabs on her until this case is resolved," the prosecutor says.

"That's ridiculous, Your Honor! My client has no intention of leaving the country or even the state for that matter," Jennifer interrupts.

The judge pauses for a moment. "Bail will be set at $1 million and the defendant will remain in the custody of the Department of Corrections on Rikers Island until bail is posted or she is acquitted of all charges. It is so ordered," he says before slamming his mallet.

Veronica looks puzzled at her attorneys. "I don't have a million dollars or even close to it. What am I going to do?" she asks.

"Don't worry. We have been through this before. For now you will have to remain in jail while we prepare your case for a jury. It is going to take a few weeks, but I can assure you that everything will be fine," Amy says.

Jennifer reassures Veronica by giving her hug. Veronica, though scared and nervous, trusts her attorneys. "We will be in contact in a few days and begin the process, OK?" Amy says sincerely.

"OK," Veronica responds before the officer arrives to take her to Rikers Island. As she is being escorted to the back of the courthouse, she looks at her attorneys talking and notices an all too familiar face sitting in the back. It's Keith watching her being taken away. He nods his head once eye contact is established, and they stare at each other until she leaves the courthouse.

What is he doing here? She thinks to herself, before the door closes on the isolated area in the back from which she came. Even after she's placed in the small room located in the courtroom, they continue looking at each other through the glass on the door.

Chapter 22

It's been a week since the separation between Veronica and Zacori. Since the tragic death of Linda, they have never been apart this long. Zacori has been forced to live in a temporary group home with other kids in need of housing until they are placed in foster care or adopted. Mr. Burns has only been granted supervised visitation on the weekends until his custody court date comes up in a few weeks.

Today he will get to see Zacori for two hours in his home, accompanied by his parole officer and a social services counselor for the first time. He has been able to keep a substantial amount of money even after his long prison sentence. His home in Chelsea is not as luxurious as his penthouse loft, but still more than the average New Yorker can afford. He sips on expensive scotch while waiting for his parole officer and Zac to arrive. Finally, there is a knock on the door. Worried about the alcohol, he hurries to finish and grabs the breath mints on the table. He reaches the door and opens it, only to be surprised by his Chinese former business associates, which quickly turns his smile into a face of fear and darkness.

"How can I help you?" he asks.

"Come on, Mr. Burns. Is this any way to treat old friends? How about we come in and catch up on things?" a gentleman suggests.

"Now is not a good time, Chin. My parole officer is on his way here with a social worker and my son to take a look at the place.

Plus, we don't have any more business. I did my time. In case you forgot, I was away for the last 13 years, alone," Mr. Burns says, looking firmly at the second gentleman wearing shades.

"I know. Don't think we forgot what you did for us. This is just a friendly visit. You know how to reach us if you need us," Chin responds before handing Mr. Burns a card with only a number on it.

"Sure!" Mr. Burns answers before stuffing the card in his front shirt pocket and closing the door. He takes a deep breath and walks back over to the bar to get another drink. He quickly downs another scotch and pauses along the bar handle, thinking deeply about what just happened. The doorbell rings. He looks himself over before opening the door for his parole officer.

"Ah, yes. Please enter, Mr. Thompson."

"Don't worry, Burns. I know your kid is coming today so this will be brief. Just let me look over the place to make sure everything is suitable for you to stay here."

"Sure, take your time. Can I offer you a drink?" ask Mr. Burns.

"Don't push it, Burns!" Thompson replies. "Looks like you're still doing pretty well after all these years. Have you been in contact with any of your old buddies?"

"I'll be honest – they came here. But, I can promise you that part of my life is done. All I want is another chance at raising my son, and that's the truth, sir."

"I believe you, Burns. I will get out of your hair. Just make sure you keep me informed on your whereabouts and do the right thing, and we will try to get you through this. By the way, the courts told me that you'll have to testify in the case against the woman you claim took your son all those years ago. Here is the date and time you must appear. You've officially been served papers," says Thompson.

"No problem. I will definitely be there, Thompson," Mr. Burns assures him.

"Let me ask you before I go. This woman took your son, raised him as her own until your release, brought him to see you when the kid was old enough to understand, and you had her put in jail like an animal. Do you feel no remorse for what you've done?"

Mr. Burns pauses for a moment. "No! The law is the law."

Thompson simply shakes his head. "That is true, Burns, but the law can also come back to bite you in the ass. Have a good day!" The two shake hands at the door as Zacori and his social worker arrive.

"This must be your son," Thompson says.

"Why, yes it is. Zacori, this is Mr. Thompson, my parole officer. This is my son, Zacori, and his social worker," says Burns.

The social worker and parole officer shake hands briefly. "Let me give you my contact information in case you need anything from me about Mr. Burns' case," says Thompson, handing the social worker his card. "Burns I will be talking to you."

Zacori and his social worker enter the apartment and sit on the couch. "You have a very nice place, Mr. Burns," she says, browsing in the living room area.

"Thank you. I only want to have the best for Zacori moving forward," he responds. "What do you think about the place, Zac? I even had the decorators set up your room if you want to take a look at it."

Zacori shrugs his shoulders, but he and the social worker go to check it out. Once they arrive at the room and open the door, they see the room is designed like an outdoor skating ramp, with autographed pictures of some of the top skaters.

"I pulled a few strings with some old friends to have some of your favorite skaters you told me about sign those tee shirts along the wall," Mr. Burns says. Zacori analyzes each shirt in absolute awe, getting more excited as he reads off the names. On the bed is a brand new skateboard autographed by Steve Caballero that really wins Zacori over.

"OH MY GOD! This is what I always wanted. Thanks, Dad. The room, the gifts – everything is amazing. Thanks so much," he says, sitting on the bed analyzing his new board.

"Only the best for you, champ," Mr. Burns replies.

"These are great gifts, Mr. Burns, and a very nice place, but we have to discuss in detail your court date coming up next week. Is there somewhere we can go to speak in private?" the social worker asks.

"Sure, we can go to the study."

"Zacori, we will be right in the back talking, OK?" Overwhelmed with the board he received, he just nods yes.

After arriving in the study, the social worker mentions to Mr. Burns that his chances of having Zacori live with him look good as long as parole approves and he keeps away from trouble. Everything seems to be working in his favor, especially after Veronica has been put out of the way in jail. Since Linda is dead, there is no one else who can stand in his way as he claims his rights to custody. They hear a knock on the door.

"Please come in, Zacori. This is your house too," Mr. Burns says.

"Ms. Jones, I'm ready to go now," he says. Ms. Jones and Mr. Burns look at each other in shock.

"But you still have three more hours in your visit with your dad," she says.

"Zac, I was hoping we could have a father and son dinner, maybe take a nice walk and talk," Mr. Burns says.

"I know, but I just want to go back to the facility," Zacori says.

"You don't like the things I got you? Your new home? Are the hats OK? We can get new things, even a new house if you'd like," Mr. Burns says.

"That's not it. The gifts are great, but they were bought to win me over. If Mom didn't teach me anything else, she taught me to work hard for things to appreciate them more. And this isn't my home; it's yours. I live in the Lower East Side, so if I am not living there with my mom, then send me back to where I was last night," Zacori says.

"But, Zacori..." Ms. Jones tries to explain, but Zacori turns his back and walks out the door.

"I am ready Ms. Jones. Later, Dad," he says. Ms Jones is speechless as she looks at Mr. Burns standing behind the desk.

"I'm sorry, Mr. Burns. Sometimes it takes kids a little bit more time to adjust, and we can't force them to stay. We will be in touch." Ms. Jones says before leaving.

Feeling powerless, Mr. Burns stares at the wall in deep thought.

Chapter 23

Trial Day 1

5 a.m.: The day begins with Veronica staring at the ceiling in her cell. It's the first day of her kidnapping trial. All night she tossed and turned, unable to sleep, anticipating how this day will turn out. Sleep isn't something she is too familiar with these days anyway, especially on a hard mattress on Rikers Island.

7 a.m.: After a quick shower, she gets breakfast in the chow hall before getting on the bus to be transported to court. Her nerves make it almost impossible to eat fully, so she has an apple and drinks some juice before returning to her cell and gathering her clothes.

10 a.m.: Arriving at court with her hands and legs shackled, she is put in a holding pen to wait for her name to be called to speak with her lawyers. Finally she is transported to a small room in the back where Amy and Jennifer are already sitting. Veronica sits in the chair thinking of how the next few hours will turn out.

"How are you doing?" Amy asks.

"For whatever it's worth, I'm exhausted. I can't stop thinking about why I'm here," Veronica responds.

"I know it's difficult, but it'll be over soon. Today we just have to stay focused on maintaining your innocence and proving to the jury that you did nothing wrong. I have to tell you that the process is going to be difficult, especially when it comes to the witnesses. I had to subpoena a few people to take the stand, some in your favor, some not.

"Who's in my favor?" Veronica asks

"We have your friend from the school. Zacori of course, as he is old enough to speak for you. And lastly, you!" says Jennifer.

"Me? Why me? Are you sure you want me to take the stand?"

"Veronica, nobody will be able to tell the jury what the last 13 years have been like, but you. They need to feel exactly the passion that made you stop your life to take care of a little boy who was not only a stranger to you, but a victim of abuse, and whose parents abandoned him," says Amy.

Veronica agrees after Amy explains things to her. "I guess you're right. I have nothing to lose anyway; I am already in jail. Who is against me?" she asks.

"Of course, Mr. Burns, who brought all this about. Your ex-husband Keith was also subpoenaed, and the last person is not really against you, but it is a social worker who will be speaking on Zacori's welfare and the laws that are against what you have done. We will prove your innocence because we believe you," says Amy.

"And if the jury finds me guilty? How many years will I be facing?" Veronica asks.

"Anywhere from 20 to 30 years on the kidnapping charge, and four years on endangering the welfare of a child," Amy answers.

"Oh my God, that's almost 35 years," Veronica cries, almost losing control of herself. Amy grabs her shoulders.

"Listen to me! I know this may be hard, and I can't imagine how you feel, but you need to get yourself together. You can't show any signs of weakness or guilt inside that courtroom. Emotions are one thing, but weakness is not acceptable. We never said this was going to be easy, but we have to win this case. We only have an hour before opening testimony, so let's go," Amy says, urging Veronica to pull it together.

Knowing her destiny is on the line, Veronica wipes her face and looks Amy in the eyes before agreeing. Silence fills the room as Veronica tries her hardest to remain tough and prepare for whatever the future may bring.

1 p.m.: The time has come for the case to begin. Veronica sits alongside her attorneys looking around the room at the faces who will decide her fate. It is a predominately Caucasian jury of six men and six women. There is one black and one Asian woman mixed into the group, but that doesn't bother her too much. The prosecution begins with their opening arguments. It is very disturbing for Veronica to hear people she doesn't even know make her out to be the worst person in the world. What is more alarming is that a few of the jurors periodically look over at her, shaking their heads in agreement. *I am a dead duck, she* thinks to herself.

After the prosecution's opening arguments they are ready to call their first witness, Mr. Burns. He enters the courtroom from the rear and proceeds to the witness stand. Once inside, he raises his right hand to take his oath. Overwhelmed with rage, Veronica can only sit and stare at him while he refuses to make eye contact. "What a coward," she mumbles before feeling Amy's knee hit her leg. She listens to him tell the judge and jury how he missed his son and was deprived of the opportunity to have a relationship with Zacori because of Veronica.

"Mr. Burns, can you explain to us how you felt the first time you saw your son after all these years?"

"I don't think I can describe that in words. I thought my son was either in foster care or killed by his mother when she took her life and the life of my unborn son," he responds. He puts his head down and takes out his handkerchief to wipe the tears from his eyes. It disgusts Veronica to see him be so phony and nonchalant about the truth, but if you tell yourself the same lie over and over again, even you begin to believe it's true. Veronica smiles watching him make his plea for Zacori.

Turning her head in the courtroom to look at the audience, she once again sees Keith sitting in the rear looking at her. Today he is dressed well and perfectly groomed in a suit, as he used to be when they first met. She doesn't want to admit it, but he is looking pretty handsome today. Quickly she cuts her eyes back to Mr. Burns when she hears the question she's waiting for.

"Mr. Burns, do you believe that the defendant purposely kidnapped your son?"

"Yes, I do," he responds.

"And why do you believe she would do such a thing?" the prosecutor asks.

"I believe the defendant purposely kidnapped my son because she is not capable of having children on her own," he says. The courtroom fills with whispers. Amy looks over to Veronica who is in complete awe. "How did you obtain this information, Mr. Burns?" the prosecutor asks.

"From her ex-husband. He told me while we were on a business trip. He told me a lot of things about her when we ventured out on business," he says.

"What did he say about her character? What kind of person was she?"

"Initially he told me that she was very promiscuous before they met, always partying and drinking with strange men in nightclubs. He even expressed to me how he had to stop her from being raped one time after she was too intoxicated to know what was going on. I personally have witnessed her in my house acting very loose with guests at a Christmas party," he says.

Veronica grabs her legal pad and writes "That's a lie!" before sliding it into Jennifer's view. Jennifer looks at her and writes "Is the baby part true?"

"Yes and no. My husband refused to test his sperm count. He even hit me when I mentioned it," she writes. Jennifer nods her head and begins to whisper to Amy.

Back on the stand, Mr. Burns sits as the prosecutor rests. It is now time for Amy to question him.

"Mr. Burns, we know that Ms. Owuso was one of your employees who just happened to be friends with your wife before she even got the job with you. Am I correct?" she asks.

"Yes, that is true," he responds.

"And she was promoted by you before your wife recognized her in the office. Is that true?"

"Yes, that's true." When she first started, she had a lot of potential. I can agree to that."

"You just finished a long jail sentence, isn't that correct? What was it, 13 years?"

"Yes."

"And what were the charges, if you can remind the court?"

"Objection, Your Honor! The witness is not the one on trial," the prosecutor yells.

"I will allow the question," says the judge.

"I did my time. This is about my son and her kidnapping him..." Mr. Burns tries to say before being interrupted by the judge.

"Answer the question!" the judge demands.

Mr. Burns' face becomes red as he is forced to say what he was convicted of. "Trafficking illegal immigrants and soliciting prostitution," he responds.

"Wow, those are some serious charges, some may say. Now, in 13 years, how many times did you provide for Zacori? Go to a game? Watch him skateboard? Played catch in the yard? Protected him from being bullied? You know, things dads do with their sons," she asks.

"I was unable to do those things," he answers.

"That's right! You were too busy being property of the state for charges that would normally endanger the welfare of a child. How soon we forget. How about this one, Mr. Burns? Isn't it true that your son was abused by the same woman you brought into this country, who just happened to be your paid mistress?"

"Yes," he answers.

"Is this the same woman you brought into your home as a nanny with your wife and son?" she asks.

Mr. Burns remains silent, staring at Amy with rage.

"Nothing yet, huh? OK, better yet, what happened to your wife, Mr. Burns?" Amy asks.

Mr. Burns clears his throat. "She committed suicide."

"Where?" Amy quickly asks.

"In Veronica's apartment," he answers.

"When?"

"During my sentencing."

"So do you believe, that it's possible, since you were going to be sent to prison for a long time, that your wife's last wishes were to leave your son in good hands?" she asks.

Mr. Burns says nothing as he stares at Amy with a look to kill. "No matter what I was going through or what my wife's wishes were, I am still his legal guardian, and in no way did she have the right to give some random nig –" Mr. Burns quickly catches himself and clears his throat. "…Even if the circumstances were challenging."

"Nigger, Mr. Burns? Cute, real cute. Good answer, by the way. But that's not why we're here. The truth is your wife committed suicide because you played her like an ass. And while you were in jail with shelter and food, heat and hot water paid for by the state, Veronica suffered and put her life on hold to raise your child. She provided him with all the things a parent should for their child and gave him the one thing neither you or your wife were able to provide for the last 13 years, and that's good ole' parental love. Isn't that right, Mr. Burns? No further questions for this witness, your Honor," Amy says before sitting in her chair and slamming her notepad on the table.

"You may step down, Mr. Burns," says the judge. Mr. Burns gets up to fix his suit jacket before stepping down and exiting the courtroom. There is nothing he can say, but it's evident that Amy has brought him to tears as he wipes his eyes with his handkerchief. Veronica sits in her chair with her hands under her chin and fingers resting over her mouth. The tears are building up, but never roll down her face. Jennifer gently rubs her back to acknowledge that she understands before court adjourns for lunch.

2 p.m.: After lunch, the prosecution is prepared to call their next witness. Things went a little better than Veronica anticipated with

Mr. Burns taking the stand, but there is one fact that remains, which is that she doesn't have the legal right to have Zacori. It is clear she didn't follow the law, but it's left to 12 jurors to decide if it was morally right. As the court officer calls Keith's name to enter the court and take the stand, Veronica can't help but to feel nervous. He promises to tell the truth, while she thinks to herself, *I heard that before*. He briefly looks over to her and makes eye contact.

"Is it OK if we call you Keith, or would you prefer to be called by your Arabic name?"

"Keith will be fine," he answers.

"How long were you married to the defendant?"

"I was with Veronica for a total of nine years married," Keith answers.

"And how was your relationship?"

"There were good times and some bad times. Like any couple we disagreed at times."

"Do you know Mr. Burns?" he asks.

"Yes. I do know Mr. Burns," says Keith.

"Do you feel he was or is capable of taking care of his son?" asks the prosecutor.

Jennifer quickly stands. "Objection, Your Honor! Questioning Mr. Burns' ability to take care of his son is pointless to this case," she says.

"Agreed. The jury will disregard the last question," he says.

"Thank you," says Jennifer.

"How was your relationship after your wife took responsibility of Zacori?" asks the prosecutor.

"It was challenging. She really wanted to get pregnant but was unable to," he responds.

"Quick question, did your wife ever consult with you about seeing the proper authorities, or even consider what she should legally do about Zacori?"

"No, she didn't. After we found Linda in her apartment dead, the letter stated that it was Linda's wishes for Veronica to take care of him. We just took the responsibility," answers Keith.

Amy looks at Veronica and writes, "Where's the letter?" Veronica shrugs as if she has no idea.

"So what you mean to tell the court that a letter was left, and that alone was enough for you and the defendant to take Zacori and never properly alert the authorities?"

"Yes! Veronica was very adamant about keeping Zacori and raising him as her own."

"Did you ever want to alert the authorities as to Zacori's whereabouts?"

"Honestly, no," Keith answers.

"So you also played a specific role in the kidnapping of this child?"

Keith pauses for moment before answering the question. "I never considered keeping Zacori with us and providing him with a stable life while his parents were not in the picture kidnapping. But if that's playing a major role in his life, then the answer is yes! I assume I did under those terms."

"No further questions, Your Honor," says the prosecutor.

Jennifer stands and approaches the witness stand. "How was your relationship with Veronica?"

"Like I said before, it had good times and some troubling times, like any other marriage."

"Where those bad times because of abuse?"

Keith adjusts himself in the chair, feeling very uncomfortable with the question. "I don't understand what you mean," he says.

"OK, how can we adjust the question for you? Abused, beaten, punched, kicked, slapped. Do those words assist you in the thinking process?"

"We had some very trying times," Keith responds.

"So your wife used her religious clothing to cover her wounds from society. Isn't that true?"

"Yes. I was very aggressive with her at times, and I deeply regret and apologize for what I put her through." He looks toward Veronica. What I did to the woman whom I loved deeply was wrong, and I understand now that her wounds may have healed but the pain will always remain. I was brainwashed into thinking that she was less than my equal and should be disciplined in a certain way," Keith says.

"I see! How would you say Veronica treated Zacori in all the years he was with her?" asks Amy.

"As if he were her child," he answers.

"I heard you mention a letter that was left on the day Linda committed suicide in Veronica's apartment. Obviously by your testimony, we know what it may have said, but do you have any idea of where that letter could be now?"

Keith looks over to Veronica before turning to the prosecutor and answers, "I'm sorry. Yes I do!" The courtroom erupts with whispers before the judge demands order. Veronica's eyes open widely as she grabs Jennifer's arm. Keith reaches into his inside pocket and pulls out two envelopes.

"Objection, Your Honor," yells the prosecutor. "That evidence was not filed with the court prior to today and has not been looked over by either counsel," he says.

"Your Honor, we believe the letter that the witness is holding can be the very proof that my client indeed acted out of good faith. Also, it states the wishes of the biological mother for my client to be the caregiver of her son after the sentencing of Mr. Burns," Amy says.

"I will allow this evidence to be presented to the court for review. Bailiff, can you please take both envelopes from the witness and present them as evidence documents A and B in the court after showing them to counsel? The letters presented in this case will be read by the witness to the court," the judge orders.

The bailiff takes the letters and presents them to Amy and the prosecutor for review, before returning to the witness stand for the letters to be read. Keith reaches into his pocket and pulls out his glasses. The courtroom is so quiet that only the wind coming through the windows can be heard.

"Your Honor, one of the letters was never opened because it was addressed to Zacori from Linda. We never opened it to see what it said. It was intended for him to have when he was old enough to understand or handle the situation," says Keith.

"I understand. Document B will be given to Zacori when the time is appropriate. For now can you please read the letter addressed to Veronica from Linda?" the judge asks.

"Sure," Keith answers. Everyone sits on the edge of their seats paying close attention as Keith begins reading. After he finishes, the prosecutor immediately questions its authenticity.

They find it highly unlikely for Keith to have the letters in his possession for 13 years, and believe that it is a tactic to gain sympathy. Veronica is teary-eyed after hearing Linda's words. With no further questions from the prosecution or defense attorneys, Keith steps down from the witness stand. With his head toward the ground, he suddenly stops next to Veronica's table and whispers "Sorry" before exiting the courtroom. She turns her head to watch him leave and yells, "I forgive you, and may God be with you, Keith." He stops but doesn't turn around. Veronica remains looking at the door, saying, "It's OK, Keith. I forgive you. I forgive you."

Chapter 24

Day 2

It's day two of the trial and the defense is calling another witness to the stand. Even after the testimonies of Keith and Mr. Burns, Amy is still focused on getting a positive outcome. "This case is far from over, and we still have a long way to go," she said after yesterday's testimony. Amy and Jennifer have been doing this a long time and have seen the best and worst of the judicial system, so Veronica trusts in her lawyers. All night she thought about Keith and what happened when he took the stand. She was shocked that he never made her out to be a horrible person, and his testimony was actually more in favor of her than anything.

He actually held on to the letter for all these years, she thinks to herself. What could have made him change? The last time they saw each other he acted as if he would have killed her. *Is he still with his other wife? What is he doing for himself these days? Is he still practicing Islam? Oh my God! Why am I thinking of Keith so much? This is ridiculous. This is the same man who almost beat me to death a few years ago.* She assumes this is just natural after not seeing someone for so long, but she has to face reality. Keith was her husband and she still loves him, but he abused her.

Before she gets herself prepared for court, there's still about an hour before the officers arrive. Veronica decides to have a conversation with the only one whom never let her down, God. She places a blanket on the floor and proceeds to wash her hands and face at the sink in her cell. She wraps her head with a scarf and kneels down on the blanket, sitting silently with her palms up and head down. If she learned anything from her time practicing Islam, she learned the correct way to pray.

Good morning God
In thee, O LORD, do I put my trust?
Let me never be ashamed.
Deliver me in thy righteousness.
Bow down thine ear to me. Deliver me speedily.
Be thou my strong rock,
For a house of defense to save me.
For thou art my rock and my fortress
Therefore for thy name leads me and guides me.
Pull me out of the net that they have laid for me
For thou art my strength.
Into thine hand I commit my spirit
Thou hast redeemed me, O LORD God of truth.
I have hated them that regard lying vanities
But I trust in the LORD.
I will be glad and rejoice in thy mercy
For thou hast considered my trouble;
Thou hast known my soul in adversities;
And hast not shut me up into the hand of the enemy
thou hast set my feet in a large room.
Have mercy upon me, O LORD, for I am in trouble:
Mine eye is consumed with grief,
Yea, my soul and my belly.
For my life is spent with grief,
and my years with sighing
my strength faileth because of mine iniquity,
and my bones are consumed.
I was a reproach among all mine enemies,
but especially among my neighbors,

and a fear to my acquaintances
they that did see me without fleeing from me.
I am forgotten as a dead man out of mind.
I am like a broken vessel.
For I have heard the slander of many.
Fear was on every side
while they took counsel together against me,
they devised to take away my life.
But I trusted in thee, O LORD.
I said, Thou art my God.
My times are in thy hand.
Deliver me from the hand of mine enemies,
and from them that persecute me.
Make thy face to shine upon thy servant
Save me for thy mercies' sake.
Let me not be ashamed, O LORD;
for I have called upon thee.
Let the wicked be ashamed,
and let them be silent in the grave.
Let the lying lips that speak grievous things
proudly and contemptuously against the righteous
be put to silence.
Oh how great is thy goodness,
which thou hast laid up for them that fear thee
which thou hast wrought for them that trust in thee
before the sons of men!
Thou shalt hide them in the secret of thy presence
from the pride of man
thou shalt keep them secretly in a pavilion
from the strife of tongues.
Blessed be the LORD
for he hath showed me his marvelous kindness in a strong city.
For I said in my haste,
I am cut off from before thine eyes
Nevertheless thou heard the voice of my supplications

when I cried unto thee
O love the LORD, all ye his saints:
for the LORD preserveth the faithful,
and plentifully rewarded the proud doer.
Be of good courage, and he shall strengthen your heart,
all ye that hope in the LORD.
Amen

After prayer, Veronica is only left with enough time to put her clothes on and await the arrival of the officers. She can't take the risk of missing the bus because she will be held in contempt for one missed court date. Today she will find out exactly when she will have to take the stand, or if it is even necessary. Her lawyers are always there before everyone else, talking and trying to reach some sort of agreement or dismissal. Nothing would make her feel better than to arrive at the court and be told she would be set free, but for now the shackles are a reminder that that decision hasn't been made yet.

She boards the bus and takes a seat next to window. There aren't too many women on the bus today going to court. Sometimes the bus ride is the highlight of the day, hearing everyone discuss their cases or giving out legal advice. Veronica can't deny that remaining in jail is beginning to get to her. Looking out the window, there isn't anything she wants more than to be the person looking at the bus instead of the person inside. It's funny how simple things as fresh air, walking in the park, listening to the birds while reading a book or just going to a local market can become the very things you miss the most, but nothing can compare to how much she misses Zacori. Not a day goes by that she doesn't think about how he's doing, if he ate or is he still going to school.

"What I wouldn't give to see him doing tricks on his skateboard right now," she thought to herself. All of the memories and thoughts in her head can only bring tears to her eyes as she continues to look at the people outside just enjoying everyday life. To be incarcerated for a little over a month is too much for her. She really can't do 30 to 40 years.

An hour later, the bus arrives at the courthouse. Veronica proceeds to the court as usual, shackled hand and foot, embarrassed as people look on. The stares become so obvious that the female officer stops her from walking.

"Are you OK?" asks the officer, looking into Veronica's eyes.

"Yes I'm fine!"

The officer obviously knows this is taking a toll on Veronica and decides to take the cuffs off her feet, placing her hands behind her back. "I know why you're here, and no matter what I may personally think, if you decide to run I will kill you," says the officer with a smile on her face.

"I don't think I will make it too far, but thank you." Veronica smiles back at the officer.

"It's OK, sister, hold your head up." Veronica walks toward the courthouse with her head up straight, strong and confident.

When she finally reaches the small room outside the courtroom, Amy and Jennifer, who both have tremendous smiles on their faces, meet Veronica. The two ladies are so happy they make Veronica smile. "What happened?" she asks.

"We have great news. Please sit down," says Amy.

"Am I being released?" asks Veronica.

"Not that great," Amy says jokingly. "We had a meeting with the DA's office, and by tomorrow we may have a plea bargain on the table."

"So what does that mean?"

"Well, it means anything from less time in prison or possible probation, depending on what both parties can agree on," Jennifer explains.

"But I thought I didn't have anything to worry about. You guys told me that, right? That's what you said," Veronica tells them.

"We know Veronica, but the hard part is getting around the fact that you didn't use the proper channels of the law to inform them you had Zacori in your custody. That may be hard to overlook," Amy explains. "Look. The defense has one more witness they will be calling today, and we will have our chance to prove your innocence. You don't have to take the plea, but if you blow trial your fate is in the hands of the jurors. Are you willing to take that risk?" Jennifer asks.

Veronica pauses to think about the risks she is about to take. Never seeing Zacori or having her freedom again crosses her mind, but she refuses to admit to a crime that she knows she didn't commit.

"I am sorry guys, but I know what I did was out of love and commitment. And if that leaves me in jail for possibly the rest of my life, then that's something I must live with. Whoever disagrees will have to deal with my God about it," Veronica says.

"Then we'll have to put you on the stand," Amy explains.

"That's fine, I am ready. Believe me I am ready," Veronica answers.

The courtroom is a little more crowded than the first day. The prosecutor calls their last and final witness, the school principal.

"Good morning, Mrs. Johnson! Just to bring you up to speed with what's going on, do you recognize the defendant?" the prosecutor asks.

"Yes."

"Under what terms did you meet the defendant?"

"She is the nanny of one of my students, Zacori Burns."

"Is this how she always introduced herself?"

"Yes! I have met with her many times to discuss any issues Zacori may have had in school, and I've seen her time and time again picking him up," she answers.

"Is this common for your students?"

"It's common for us to talk with the nannies about what goes on with the kids. In most cases, all we do is discuss affairs with the nannies because the parents of our children are either traveling on business or too busy to come to the school," she answers.

"Do you keep any records signed by parents in order for the school to be able to talk to these nannies?"

"Of course," she says.

"Do you have a signed consent form from either parent of Zacori Burns?"

"Yes I do! Mrs. Johnson states before submitting the form. The prosecutor takes the form and looks over it carefully. He passes it to Amy, who also looks over it with Jennifer. Amy writes a large question mark on a pad before passing it over to Veronica to look at. Veronica responds by writing, "Damn."

"Do you see a signature on this form?"

"Yes. On the bottom right, the form is signed by Linda Burns."

"And how many years ago was this form signed by Mrs. Burns?"

"It was signed two years ago," the principal answers.

"Two years ago. What would you say if I told you that not only did Mrs. Burns commit suicide 13 years ago, but there was no record of Mr. Burns having a second wife who could legally call themselves Mrs. Burns?"

"I would say someone forged the form," Mrs. Johnson answers.

"And who was listed as the person to make all decisions in the absence of either parent?"

The principal looks at the paper before answering, "Veronica Owuso."

"Do you see Mrs. Owuso in the courtroom today? If so, please point to her," he asks.

The principal turns toward Veronica and immediately points in her direction.

"Please let the record show that the witness has pointed to the defendant. Ladies and gentlemen of the jury, what we have here is a woman who never properly informed the authorities of the whereabouts of Zacori Burns, but has also continued to lie about her relationship with him. No further questions."

Amy taps her pencil thinking of the perfect sequence of questions. She stands and calmly walks over to the witness stand.

"Do you love children, Mrs. Johnson?"

"Yes, I have dedicated my life to them."

"Do you ever go above and beyond your job description for certain kids?"

"Yes, I do."

"Have you ever seen Zacori Burns mistreated, undernourished or misbehaving?" Amy asks.

"No. He is a very respectful child," the principal answers.

"So would it be accurate to say he was well taken care of and raised to be respectful?"

"Yes."

"And is it common for a child to call their nanny mom or mother sometimes in the absence of the parents?"

"Yes. I have witnessed many children get confused as to who their real parents are. Kids care for the ones taking care of them, and sometimes they may call their non-biological loved ones mom or dad."

"So here is my question to you, Mrs. Johnson. As a woman who has dedicated her life to children and even admitted that you do extra to protect the welfare of kids who are not biologically yours, would you have done the same as Ms. Owuso if you were in her position?"

Mrs. Johnson looks at the jury and answers yes with no hesitation or interruption.

"No further questions, Your Honor," says Amy.

"Unbelievable!" the prosecutor yells, throwing his pencil on the table.

The principal leaves the witness stand and waves toward Veronica before leaving the courtroom. As she is the last witness for the prosecution, the trial is almost over. The judge decides to adjourn court for the day and begin fresh tomorrow with the defense. All the lawyers begin to gather their belongings after the jury is dismissed, and Amy and Jennifer give Veronica a warm hug before she is handcuffed to be sent back to jail.

"See you guys later," she says before the bailiff escorts her out. Sitting in the rear of the courtroom is the district attorney who approaches the defense attorney's table.

"I need to speak with you guys in my office. Is 3 o'clock good?" she asks.

"Yes, sure," they respond.

Chapter 25

Family Court

Meanwhile, the custody hearing for Mr. Burns is beginning in family court. The magistrate looks over the papers and directs her questions over to Mr. Burns.

"I see that you were incarcerated for the past 13 years and released early for good behavior, correct?" she asks.

"Yes ma'am. That is correct."

"I also see that your son was being cared for by a woman who is currently incarcerated on charges of kidnapping, which you actually filed once released. Is this correct?"

"Yes ma'am, it is."

"Did you know her?"

"Yes I did."

"Was your son abused?"

"Not to my knowledge."

"Neglected?"

"Not to my knowledge."

"Then why, if you were unable to do your job as a parent, would you blame the person who was able to?" she asks.

Mr. Burns pauses and looks at the magistrate, annoyed at the question. "Because she broke the law."

"She broke the law," the magistrate chuckles. "And you were his angel. What a country we live in. Anyway, we are here to have a custody hearing for your son, correct? It is the duty of the court to make sure Zacori has the best care and lives under the best circumstances. Now, I have gone over your parole officer's records and evaluation, but also those of the social worker in charge of your case. Mr. Burns, why should I grant you custody of your son?"

"The only answer I can give you is that I made my mistakes and paid society back for them, but I never mistreated my son or intended for him to be apart from me. I am still able to provide him with a better life and secure his future," Mr. Burns explains.

"I see. As a man with what I assume is a lot of political and business influence, why would you come to this courtroom without a lawyer?"

"I am not here to prove my innocence. I just want my son back."

"The court will grant you full custody with unannounced visits from case workers and monthly reports to the Department of Parole. What I want you to understand is that even if I don't agree with how you went about regaining custody of your son, I do agree that a child should be with their biological parents if it's permissible. Just to inform you, at the age of 16 in New York state your son will be able to be on his own if he is able to prove to the court that he can care for himself. Do you understand that?"

"Yes I do," Mr. Burns answers.

"Case dismissed. Mr. Burns will receive custody of his son immediately under the provisions of my orders. Please wait outside for all required paperwork," the magistrate says before Mr. Burns exits the courtroom smiling.

~

It's mid-afternoon when Amy and Jennifer arrive at the DA's office as they were instructed earlier.

"Ladies, I am glad that you were able to meet me on short notice. I have some concerns about how this case is going. First, I would like to hear your opinions," she says.

"As we all know, the defense just rested and we think it's going very well. We ran into a few surprises with jury selection, but the ex-husband really gave us an advantage with the letters from Burns' deceased wife," says Amy.

Jennifer says, "I am more worried about when we have to present our case. Will Veronica be convincing enough for a verdict of not guilty to be the only decision?"

"Exactly! Do I agree this woman should be set free? Of course. But a jury of predominately men and a plea bargain off the table are not helpful to her case. I am totally aware of the efforts you have put forth, but I am afraid she will have to do some jail time if we blow this," the DA explains.

"Is there anything we can do that will help us convince the jury of her innocence?" asks Amy.

"The only thing that will have to be done is to put the kid on the stand, and then have Veronica tell her story. I may be able to help you with something, but I will have to make a few calls and get back to you. As much as this is going to be hard to hear, this case will be wrapping up soon. It's all or nothing moving forward. The more witnesses you call to the stand, the more you may hurt her case. You only need Veronica and the kid to convince the jury of the love they have for each other, but remember: never speak on how she gained custody. Only speak on what she has done to give him a life outside the system," the DA explains.

"And if that looks like it isn't going to work?" Jennifer asks.

"Then, she should have taken the plea."

Chapter 26

Day 3

It's day three of the case and everyone sits in silence before the judge arrives. Today Veronica will see Zacori for the first time since they were separated. Her attorneys have informed her that the case will last no longer than a day or two, but hasn't been given too many details on what to expect when the jury reaches a verdict. As far as Veronica is concerned, the possibility of jail time was never out of the picture; she only worried about how much time she would face. After the judge arrives, the prosecution informs him they have finished calling all witnesses and the ball is in the defense's hands. Amy stands.

"The defense calls Zacori Burns to the stand," she says.

Suddenly the rear doors open and all eyes are toward the back. Veronica turns her head with her eyes wide open anticipating his arrival. As he enters, she smiles then cries.

"Mom!" he yells over to her. He tries to reach over and hug her before being stopped by the court officers. "Mom! I am so sorry, Mom. I am sorry!"

Veronica raises her arms to reach for him. "It's OK, Zac. I know it wasn't your fault." Zacori stands in the witness booth as he takes an oath, his right hand raised with tears flowing from his eyes looking over to Veronica the whole time. Amy stands near the edge of the desk wiping tears with a tissue. Looking over to the jury, she realizes the jury's had the same reaction, especially the women. The men are not as emotional but they seem a little uncomfortable. Jennifer runs her hand along Veronica's back to give her support.

"What an amazing word, 'mom.' Excuse me, ladies and gentlemen of the jury. I was just as taken aback as you were with that overwhelming expression of love I just witnessed," Amy says.

She walks over to the witness stand and hands Zacori a box of tissues. "Hi, Zacori. Are you OK?"

"I am OK," he answers.

"Have you been sleeping well these days, eating well?"

"Objection! She is leading the witness your Honor," the prosecutor yells.

"I am only asking about the welfare of the witness. Not only has my client's life been rearranged, but the witness' has also. He is why we're here," Amy responds.

The judge doesn't hesitate. "Overruled! You may answer the question, young man."

"I guess I've been eating pretty well."

"How are things with your father after all these years away from him?"

"It's different. I have things I never had before living with my mom," he answers.

"Things like what?"

"More freedom to do what I want."

"Freedom. It's funny that you say freedom, Zacori. When you were with your mom – is it OK for me to call Veronica your mom?"

"That's fine. She is the only mom I've ever known," he answers.

"Did Veronica, your mom, ever tell you that she was your biological mother?"

"No. She always told me my real mom was in heaven. When I was younger, I prayed to her every night. Mom made that a priority before I went bed, until I got older and it was left up to me," he says.

"And what did she tell you about your father?"

"All I can really remember is that she didn't know exactly where he was but found him when she was asked to."

"We're you ever denied anything growing up?" Amy asks.

"No! I love my mom. I wish I was still with her." Zacori's words begin to crack as her tries to hold back from crying. "It's my fault she is in jail now. I was tricked into telling my father information to set her up."

"I am sorry. Do you need a few minutes to get yourself together?" she asks while passing the box of tissue to him. "Take your time Zacori. I know this is very hard for you."

"I'm fine," he says.

"I only have a few more questions. Who is this woman that we keep referring to, and if you see her in the courtroom, can you point her out?"

Zacori immediately points in Veronica's direction. There she is. There is my mom."

"Let me know if I say something that's incorrect. You went to the best schools New York had to offer, were never physically or emotionally abused, and encouraged to do your best at everything you put your mind to. I hear that you're an excellent skateboarder. You were always given the best. Is that accurate to say?" she asks.

"Yes it is," he answers.

"Do you wish for any other mom over Veronica?" she asks.

"No! I'll give up everything I have now to be back with her."

"No further questions, Your Honor," Amy says.

"Hello, Zacori," says the prosecutor as he begins to walk toward the jury box. I understand that you have been through a lot over the last few years, and especially the last two months, so I only have two questions for you. Is that OK?" He asks.

"Sure."

"My first question: How old are you now, 15 to 16, is that correct?"

"Yes."

"So it's pretty clear that you understand what is going on here?"

"Yes, I do."

"So do you feel Veronica Owuso broke the law of the state of New York? You don't have to answer right away, but when you do, give us the truth, please."

Zacori pauses, unsure of how to properly answer the question. He looks over to Veronica, who nods her head for him to be honest. Zacori leans toward the microphone and says yes.

"No further questions, Your Honor," the prosecutor says before sitting back in his chair.

"The witness may be excused," says the judge. The court officer proceeds to escort Zacori from the witness stand to benches in the rear of the court where Mr. Burns is waiting. As they walk down the aisle, Mr. Burns extends his arms to offer Zacori a hug.

"I am proud of you, son," he says. Zacori aggressively stops the hug and yells, "I hate you!" before storming out of the courtroom. The jury silently looks at each other after observing the interaction between father and son. Mr. Burns, humiliated by what just happened, can only fix his suit jacket and exit the courtroom.

"Order! Order!" the judge's voice echoes throughout the courtroom.

Jennifer calls Veronica to the stand. Veronica rises slowly and takes a deep breath as she walks toward the witness stand. The bailiff swears her in and she sits. This is it for her, the last testimony or statement she can make to convince this jury that she should be set free. After two months in jail and three days of trial, the time has come to tell her story. She tells herself to stay calm and tell the truth before Jennifer asks the first question.

Carefully Jennifer places pictures of Veronica and Zacori over the years on a stilt in the courtroom. The pictures are cheerful and reflect the happy times they had. Veronica smiles as she embarks on the memories.

"Good times, huh? After all the things you were going through, how did you manage to never give up?" asks Jennifer.

"I guess I never thought about it because Zacori became my life as soon as Linda died."

"We heard Zacori's testimony not too long ago and something dawned on me. Not one time did he call you Veronica. Is that something you instilled in him since he was young?"

"I never told or tried to convince Zacori I was his mother. He just one day decided to call me mom, and even with me telling him about his real mother in his later years, he never stopped," Veronica answers.

"Is he your child?"

"Of course not, but that doesn't mean I don't think of him as my son. All I had in my life was that young man since he was three years old. I lost myself in order to love him better, then had to figure myself back out in order to raise him. "That's just how it is when you love someone," she answers.

"If you the chance to do it all over again, would you have done things differently?" asks Jennifer.

"I'm sorry, but I don't know how to exactly answer that."

"What I am trying to ask is do you feel raising him all these years was a mistake?"

"The only honest mistake I made was getting in touch with Mr. Burns when he was in prison."

"I have no further questions for the defendant," Jennifer says before sitting back in her chair.

The prosecutor twirls his pen between his fingers. "This case isn't about doing the right thing or having good intentions. It is about the law. Now that you are aware of these laws, do you feel you broke any of them?" he asks.

"Yes, I did," Veronica, answers. Amy drops her pen, surprised by Veronica's answer.

"Which laws did you break?" he asks.

"I should have never forged the signature on his school records," she answers.

The prosecutor begins to chuckle, amused by her answer. "Is that all? Is that all you feel you are guilty of? What about kidnapping?"

"Well, my responsibility was to make sure I took care of him as if he was one of my own, and that meant even if I had to lie to send him to the best school or make sure he stayed with the friends he knew all his life. I never took Zacori away from his world or immediate circle. I just struggled to maintain it," she answers.

"But you unlawfully took a child, forged documents, and still sit here and claim your innocence?" he asks, increasing his volume.

Veronica remains calm and poised. "Yes!" she answers.

"Is it possibly you took Zacori because you were never able to produce children?"

"That's not true. It was my husband who refused to go to the doctor to have himself checked. I was able to years ago," she answers.

"Really? I hate to be the bearer of bad news, Ms. Owuso but your ex-husband Keith has been very busy over the years. He not only has three children in his native country, but also has since fathered two children in the past two years by wife number four. Are you sure it's still him?" he asks.

Veronica simply chuckles at the news she just received and adjusts herself in the witness chair. Looking around the courtroom, she fixes her blouse and holds her head up before answering. "I can't speak of my husband's promiscuous behavior and out of wedlock children, but what I can tell you is that even through the physical and verbal abuse I put up with over the years, I stayed loyal to my husband and faithful to the vows I made to God. My husband will be judged for his actions, but my inability to have children will never be the reason I raised my friend's child when she killed herself. I could have walked away and followed your laws, but wouldn't he have just been another statistic? Or is that what the system wants, more children placed in it instead of being raised with love? Did I break a law? Yes. But it was broken for love, the same love of a grandmother who raises all her kids' children without reporting it."

The prosecutor remains silent with a devilish smirk on his face. He slowly claps his hands and walks toward the witness stand. "Great speech with terrific comparisons, but I only need you to clarify one thing for me. You have admitted that you have broken the law, is that correct?"

"Yes, I broke the law," she answers.

"No further questions, Your Honor," says the prosecutor as he smiles all the way back to his chair. Amy and Jennifer remain sitting in their chairs, shocked at what they just heard with looks of defeat on their face. Veronica stands and walks back to her seat showing no regrets, though what she said could land her in jail. She notices Amy staring at her through the corner of her eye. "Sometimes people just want to hear the truth," she says without moving her head. After the closing arguments, the judge orders the jury to return to the assigned room until they are able to reach a verdict.

The courtroom slowly empties and Veronica is placed back in cuffs to be escorted to the holding cell. Amy assures her they will come for her as soon as a verdict is reached.

It's been three hours and no verdict has been rendered yet. Veronica sits in the cell with her palms sweating from nervousness, thinking about her testimony. In her heart she knows she said the right thing when asked if she committed a crime, but by the smirk on the prosecutor's face it may come back to hurt her. *Does it really matter?* She thinks to herself. There is nothing outside of prison waiting for her anyway. Her parents have passed away and she hasn't spoken to her sister in years. Zacori will be back with his father and she's never had friends, so her world started and will end the same - alone. No matter the jury's decision, her family and friends are gone. *Maybe going to prison won't be so bad. At least I will always have people around me,* she thinks to herself trying to find some humor in the thought of remaining in prison.

Hearing footsteps coming down the hallway, she focuses her attention on the light coming in through the bottom of the door. As each step comes closer, her heartbeat gets faster, causing her breaths to become shallower and her hands to tremble with fear. It is time for Veronica to meet her fate.

Is she going to prison for the rest of her life, or will she be a free woman? The door opens and the court officers inform her that a verdict has been reached. There is no time to pray now, so Veronica merely looks to the sky hoping God is still watching and hearing her payers. It is the longest walk ever down the hallway to the courtroom. The closer to the courtroom doors she gets, the more her teeth chatter. Veronica asks the officers if they can stop, to which they agree. After a few breaths, she raises her head and alerts the officers that she's ready. The doors open. The room is crowded with lawyers, jurors, onlookers and faces from the school where she worked. Even the DA is waiting to hear the verdict. Veronica stands next to Amy and Jennifer as they await the decision.

"Has the jury reached a decision?" asks the judge.

"Yes we have, Your Honor," the foreman answers.

The defense team joins hands. "On the charges of endangering the welfare of a child, how do you find the defendant?" asks the judge.

"We the jury find the defendant guilty, Your Honor."

Amy and Jennifer look up in shock as the guilty verdict is read. Veronica only smiles and nods her head.

"On the charges of kidnapping, how do you find the defendant?"

"We find the defendant not guilty."

Amy and Jennifer exhale with relief, knowing the more serious charge has been dismissed. Amy puts her arms around Veronica, who remains calm and patient after hearing the verdict. "What does that mean?" she asks.

"It means you won't be going to jail for the rest of your life," Amy assures her.

"I would rather be guilty of both than to have anyone believe I put Zacori's life in danger in any way, but I am thankful.

"Ladies and gentlemen of the jury, the court thanks you for your service. You are dismissed," orders the judge.

"We will adjourn until sentencing one week from today. The defendant will remain in the custody of the Department of Corrections until then. Court's dismissed."

"We have a meeting with the district attorney tomorrow to discuss exactly what we can do to get you out of this. We'll be down to the jail immediately after to inform you of our progress, OK? You'll be fine. The worst part is over," says Jennifer before hugging Veronica.

A few hours later in the district attorney's office, the lawyers and judge meet to discuss the case and possibly entering another plea bargain deal. The DA remains behind her desk while the three attorneys sit beside one another.

"Is there anything the state can do to reduce any possibility of jail time?" Amy asks.

"That's ridiculous. The jury may have let her walk on the most severe charge, but we can get a one-to-three on the endangerment charge?" the prosecutor interrupts.

"So you still want to give her the max on the smallest count? That will never happen," Amy responds.

"None of what you're asking is relevant at this point for either party. I just got off the phone with Judge Grant in immigration. It seems that he received an anonymous call about our friend Veronica's legal status in this country," says the DA. "She hasn't received citizenship yet, and under NY state law, any illegal immigrant with a guilty verdict has grounds for deportation. As bad as I also wanted to see her walk, I am sorry ladies, but my hands are tied on this one. I have made an agreement with immigration that no jail time will be rendered, but in return she will be housed under supervision until deported. That was the best I could do," explains the DA.

Both Amy and Jessica are initially saddened by the news, hoping that Veronica would've been released and able to begin a new life, but this is the only option for her. She will return to her native Ghana after all these years to start over.

"This girl doesn't have any family back in Ghana. How are we going to tell her about starting all over where nothing exists for her anymore?" Jennifer asks.

"We have to just be honest and hope she understands we did our best. The only good news is that she won't spend the rest of her life locked up in a cage like an animal," says Amy.

"Maybe we should wait until sentencing next week to tell her," the DA suggests.

"No! It's better for her to at least try to start planning what she will do, instead of being caught by surprise," says Amy.

Back at the jail, the ladies discuss Veronica's options when she gets deported. Veronica is obviously upset by the news, but is relieved that she will spend no time in prison. All she is able to do is hold her head in her hands while trying to think of a plan.

"I have no idea of what I am going to do back in Ghana. I haven't been there in so long, and there's no one for me there or a place to live," she says. Together they sit trying to figure out some sort of contingency plan for Veronica after she is deported.

"Do you have anything saved?" Amy asks.

"I only have maybe a few hundred dollars saved, no more than a thousand," she replies.

"What about your ex-husband? I am sure we can put in for alimony, especially after his testimony of abuse," Jennifer suggests.

"No! Absolutely not. My ex-husband has had his issues, but he has done enough," Veronica insists.

"Veronica! This man abused you for years. You don't feel that you are entitled to some of his finances? That's the least he can do until you get on your feet," says Jennifer.

"And I say again, he has done enough. Who would have ever thought he would still finance Zacori's school even after I left, or hold onto a letter that was used to give me my freedom? It may not be freedom here in the U.S., but it's not life in prison. He has done enough," she emphasizes.

"I'm sorry this didn't work out the way we promised, and if I was able to do more I would. It won't be a long process from here and you probably will be deported immediately after sentencing in a week. If you ever need anything or just want to talk, you know how to reach us." Amy extends her arms to hug Veronica. Jennifer follows right behind her with a hug before they exit and leave Veronica inside. She looks toward the sky and says "Thank you."

Chapter 27

Back Home

Streaks of sunlight beam through the window curtains, revealing small dust crystals floating in the room. The sound of birds singing and wind chimes outside the window awakens Veronica inside her small house in the town of Busua, Ghana. She was able to patch up her parents' old house with the money that was given to her before she was deported 11 years ago. It isn't the best and definitely needs a lot of work, but it is bigger and better than a cell. She makes her morning coffee with saltine crackers and sits on her porch watching the beautiful sunrise in the African sky.

Every morning she sits on the porch and thinks about her Zacori – what kind of young man he has grown to be, if he's graduated from college yet, how he looks. She reminisces about the good and bad times she had in America. From time to time even Keith has crossed her mind, along with Agnes, whom she assumes has probably passed away by now.

She can see a small dust cloud in the distance coming up the road. The village is not very large and located somewhat in the country, so it isn't hard to notice when a guest is coming. Usually cars continue driving past, but it seems that today one is coming directly toward her house. She stands up slowly, blocking the sun with her hands trying to get a better view of who it could be. The car finally arrives next to the house when the driver, a tall white gentleman carrying a package, steps out in his messenger's uniform.

"Hi, I have a delivery for Veronica Owuso," he says.

"Well, I'm Veronica Owuso," she responds.

"Can you sign here ma'am? I have two letters to give you today, but I was instructed that you must read the first one before I give you the second," he says.

"Can you tell me who they're from? Not many people know I live here," she asks.

"I am not sure myself, but I do know they are from New York," he says.

"New York? Wow! I haven't talked to or seen anyone from there in 11 years now. Well, you may as well have a seat, since you have to wait for me to finish reading anyway. Can I offer you something to drink, maybe some coffee or water?" she asks.

"No, thank you, I'm fine."

She opens the envelope and pulls out the letter, which reads:

Dear Mom,

I hope by the time this letter reaches you that you are in good health and spirits. I have searched for many years to locate you after we were separated over 10 years ago. There is not a day that goes by that I don't think about your beautiful smile and amazingly good heart. I am sorry for all the things that have happened to you. For a long time I felt solely responsible as the person who hurt the one who loved me the most. I know who raised me and sacrificed her life in order for me to have one. There is not a mountain I won't move to get closer to you or ocean I can't swim to find you. I know that by now you are probably thinking of what kind of man your son has become. Well, I graduated from college with a degree in business management and am now establishing my own company manufacturing skateboards for high-end clients. I hope one day that we will be able to sit and talk or take a

walk through the park like old times, but for now I will just continue my search for you and pray that when I am finally able to see you, you won't hate me. I will always love you, and will never forget all that you have done for me.
Your loving son, Zacori

Veronica sits in the chair after reading the letter and looks toward the sun, which makes her tears look golden coming down her face. "He never forgot me, God! He never forgot me!" she says repeatedly as she smells the paper hoping to just get a scent of him. She walks off the porch into the front yard and raises her head to the sky with her arms extended and screams with joy, "He didn't forget me!" The messenger comes off the porch and comforts Veronica with a hug. She drops in his arms, exhausted from joy.

"Are you OK?" he asks.

"I'm sorry, young man, but this is the best news I have ever received in my life. My son was taken away from me years ago by his father, and he was all I had. To know that he still thinks about me every day as I do him is a blessing." She desperately opens the envelope to check for an address. "Do you have a return address? I have to write him back immediately," she says.

"Well, I don't really know what this letter is, but maybe it can help you," he says. She grabs the letter from him; anxious to see if there is something she can contact Zacori with. Her eyes open wide, she pulls a small piece of paper from the envelope and looks at the letter with a check wrapped inside. The letter reads:

I can never repay you for what you have given me. I am 27 now and have inherited the trust fund left to me by my father. I am not trying to buy your love or give you a handout, but there is no one in the world I would rather have this money more than you. Thank you for loving me unconditionally and being there when everyone gave up. I will always love you, Zac. She looks at the check in the amount of $23 million and falls to her knees, covering her mouth.

"I can't believe this. I must be dreaming. This just can't be real. Am I dreaming?" she asks.

"No, Mom! This is real," a voice says coming from behind her. She slowly turns and faces the messenger who is standing with his arms open waiting to embrace her. Pausing to take a good look at the young man, Veronica begins to touch his face to see if he's real while wiping his tears.

"Yes, Mom, it's me, Zacori," he says, hugging her tightly and lifting her off the ground. "I never forgot about you. I just had to find you," he says.

Together they stand, embracing one another on Veronica's porch, mother and son reunited years of pain, trials and tribulations.

49624601R00115

Made in the USA
Charleston, SC
29 November 2015